SON OF
GOD

SON OF GOD

ROMA DOWNEY
AND
MARK BURNETT

New York Boston Nashville

FaithWords
Hachette Book Group
237 Park Avenue
New York, NY 10017

www.faithwords.com

Printed in the United States of America

RRD-C

First Edition: February 2014
10 9 8 7 6 5 4 3 2 1

FaithWords is a division of Hachette Book Group, Inc.
The FaithWords name and logo are trademarks of
Hachette Book Group, Inc.

The Hachette Speakers Bureau provides a wide range of authors for speaking events. To find out more, go to www.hachettespeakersbureau.com or call (866) 376-6591.

The publisher is not responsible for websites (or their content) that are not owned by the publisher.

ISBN: 9781455585830

CONTENTS

Chapter One   *Hope*   *1*

Chapter Two   *Mission*   *21*

Chapter Three   *Betrayal*   *65*

Chapter Four   *Deliverance*   *101*

Chapter Five   *New World*   *135*

CHAPTER ONE

HOPE

In the beginning was the word. And the word was with God. And the word was God. He was with God in the beginning. He was there in paradise with Adam and Eve. He was there with Noah in the Great Flood. He was there with Abraham when he was chosen. He was there when Moses led our people out of Egypt. In the struggle for the promised land he was always by our side. He was the light shining in the darkness.

Then He came into the world, the word became flesh and made his dwelling among us.

I am John. And I was one of his followers. After what I saw, how could I not be?

A star unlike any other shines brightly in the night sky. Just outside Babylon a wise astrologer, Prince Balthazar, steps out from his tent into the dark night. He is wealthy beyond measure, dressed in fine silk robes. With a noble grace he looks to the heavens. Speaking to anyone and no one he recites, "A star shall come out of Jacob," from memory, the Book of Numbers. "And a scepter shall rise out of Israel." A smile erupts upon his distinguished face. Balthazar is certain this star portends the arrival of a great leader. And with that he gathers his guards and attendants, all hurriedly packing his belongings. Balthazar mounts his camel. He is bound for Jerusalem, eager to be met with Good News.

In Bethlehem, outside of Jerusalem, a baby is born. Joseph, a carpenter from Nazareth, holds a tiny newborn baby boy up to the light. A smile of wonder crosses his face, for he has never known such joy. He brings the child to Mary, his wife. As she holds her son, the baby Jesus, her face transforms from tired and drained to radiant joy.

A crowd starts to gather. The star that set Balthazar toward Jerusalem has led many others to this very site. The same angelic intervention that brought Mary and Joseph to Bethlehem has also spread the news to those who need to hear it most: locals, shepherds, neighbors, and ordinary people. These are the ones whom Jesus has come to save, and for them to be standing in this small barn on this cold night is a moment unlike any other time. They are witnessing the dawning of a new era—the fulfillment of the new covenant between God and humanity.

Prince Balthazar, atop an adorned camel, greets and falls into step with two Nubian wise men. They ride elegantly on their camels, ecstatic about the prospect of meeting this great new savior. Not one of them completely realizes who Jesus is and what he represents, but on this night when a star has led them to the small town of Bethlehem, they feel at the center of the universe.

In the grotto, where Mary and Joseph hug their newborn, the crowd offers prayers and small gifts to the child. Some bow, while others weep with joy. A young shepherd steps forward to offer something far more precious: a lamb.

Joseph is thankful, but the truth is that he doesn't fully understand the gift. He smiles at Mary. She cannot stop staring at Jesus. Mary has never seen anything so precious, nor anything that fills her heart with such love.

A reflection near the grotto door catches Joseph's attention. His smile fades. The mass of farmworkers, children, and shepherds part as royal attendants quietly and very efficiently clear a path. The crowd backs away, their eyes lowered in deference.

Joseph is uneasy. The last thing he wants is trouble.

Balthazar steps forward. He has changed into his finest robes and wears a gold headdress. His behavior is not regal, however. "I am humbled," he murmurs, as he drops to his knees. He has brought gifts for the newborn child. Balthazar looks to Mary and says to her, "Lady, I believe your son is the chosen king of his people." Joseph realizes that he should bow to Balthazar, but before he can, Balthazar prostrates himself on the ground. "What is his name?" he asks Mary.

Mary gently kisses her child on the forehead. "Jesus," she tells Balthazar, surprised to see that the Nubians have also come to see their child. "His name is Jesus." These fine kings all bow down on the dirty ground before the newborn Jesus.

The crowd departs well into the night. Mary cradles Jesus, and Joseph wraps his new family in his embrace. They drift off into a blissful sleep.

Jewish Land. Jewish people. Our Jewish Nation, under Roman Rule. Occupied and oppressed, those who spoke out were crushed. We craved a savior. A messiah.

A tall man pulls water from a deep clear well. Jesus has been without water for many days. As he sips the water carefully, his body fills with replenishment. The wind blows, whipping through the backstreets of the small town, Nazareth. The man smiles. He is home, for a purpose.

An older woman clothed in a simple blue dress, apron, and shawl wrapped around her head kneads bread in her small home. Her face sprinkled with flour does not hide her beauty.

"Mary!" she hears yelled through her window. "He's back!"

Mary turns to the window.

"Who?" Mary calls back.

"Jesus!" Mary looks up to God and gives thanks before tearing off her apron and heading for the door.

A crowd rushes toward the synagogue. Mary opens the door to see Jesus, her son, standing before the congregation, reading from the Torah.

"The Spirit of the Lord is upon me," Jesus begins. The synagogue is small and cramped, filled with dozens of faces looking back at him. He sees Mary entering through the door at the back, a smile of pride on her face as she sees her son.

It is normal for members of the congregation to read lessons aloud on the Sabbath, and reading the words of the prophet Isaiah is common, but it's clear from his confidence and knowledge that Jesus is no mere member of the congregation, or even a learned student of scripture. He is the teacher. The ultimate teacher. He speaks the words of a distant prophet as though he has written the words himself. " 'He has anointed me to preach good news to the poor. Everyone who has eyes will open them and see, and those who have ears will pay attention. He has sent me to proclaim freedom for the prisoners. And to proclaim the year of the Lord's favor.' " Jesus rolls up the scroll. He grasps it firmly in his right hand as he looks out over the synagogue. "Today," he proclaims, "this scripture is fulfilled in me."

There is a collective grasp. Jesus' behavior is not usual. These words are blasphemy.

Mary's smile is replaced by a look of worry and concern. A pang of fear shoots through her heart, knowing what is sure to come next. Time slows as the weight of her son's words press down on the congregation.

Then the room explodes. "Who do you think you are?" one man in the audience screams.

"How dare you stand there pretending to be the Messiah?" demands another.

Mary tries to force her way through the crowd, hoping to protect her son. But the mass of the congregation has erupted into a rage. The crowd empties out of the synagogue and into the streets after Jesus, meaning to punish him for his blasphemous words. She is terrified. But he has slipped away, and neither Mary nor the congregation can find him anywhere. Mary is relieved; for the time being, at least, he is safe. Her knees grow weak, and she sinks to the ground. "Keep going, my son," she whispers, knowing that Jesus will somehow hear her words.

Mary's fears are well founded. For she knows, just as Jesus knows, that they live in a world where making waves and challenging the status quo is met with unrelenting violence.

———

On a body of water far more turbulent than the Jordan River, three fishermen—Peter, James, and John—finish a long night of trying to fill their nets. They have nothing to show for it. They guide their boats to shore, looks of exhaustion smearing their faces.

They care little for the concerns of prophets or kings, or Rome, or the brutal methods of Herod Antipas's soldiers. They live in Galilee, the same area as Jesus, and their fishing village of Capernaum is also a sleepy backwater. The routine of their lives is simple, predictable: fish all night, mend nets in the daytime, sleep, and then fish some more. They are happy, despite these nights where the nets come back without a single fish to show for hours of backbreaking labor— casting their heavy nets into the sea, then hauling them back in, hand over hand. Fishing is what they do.

As the fishermen guide their boats up onto the sandy beach, a distant figure can be seen walking their way. Jesus' incendiary appearance in the Nazareth synagogue was a sign that he needs to preach to people who have not known him all their lives.

Peter, the most burly and rough of the fishermen, notices Jesus watching their labors. Andrew, Peter's brother, has taken it upon himself to help pull the boats ashore, and to drag the heavy nets up onto the beach to dry. Peter pretends not to notice Jesus, though it's hard not to. Andrew, a well-meaning and bright young man, is clearly captivated by Jesus.

"Who's that?" Peter finally says in a gruff tone.

"John says he is the Messiah."

"Oh, really? Can he teach you to look after your boat instead of leaving me to do it? And can he teach you to find fish?"

"Yes, I can," Jesus replies.

Peter glares at him. His hands are great mitts, calloused and rough from years at sea. His face is lined and sunburned. His back aches from hauling nets. The last thing he needs is a "teacher" to tell him how to fish.

But before he can stop him, Jesus walks over to Peter's boat, takes hold of the hull and shoves it back out into the water.

"Hey!" Peter barks, staring with openmouthed incredulousness at the sheer nerve of this stranger who clearly knows nothing about fishing, for if he did, he'd know this is not the time of day to catch anything. "What do you think you're doing? That's my boat. And you're not allowed to launch it all by yourself."

"You'd better help me then," Jesus calmly replies.

Peter runs into the water and grabs the hull. But Jesus won't be stopped. He looks Peter in the eye and keeps pushing the boat out into the Sea of Galilee. Something in that look startles Peter. He doesn't know whether he's looking into the eyes of a madman or the eyes of a king. But something in his gut—and Peter is well known for his intuition and discretion—tells him to do as Jesus orders. Peter stops trying to pull the boat back toward shore and starts shoving it out to sea. When the water is waist deep he pulls himself up into the boat. Jesus climbs on board, too.

"What are we doing here?" Peter asks.

"Fishing."

Peter stares into those eyes one more time. "There are no fish out here."

"Peter," says Jesus, "I can show you where to find fish. What have you got to lose?"

Peter reaches for his nets, preparing to cast.

Jesus shakes his head. "Go farther," he commands.

Peter looks at him. "You've never fished here. So listen when I tell you—there are no fish out there at this time of day."

"Please."

So Peter guides his boat into deeper waters.

"Blessed are they who hunger after righteousness," Jesus says. "For they shall be filled."

"Who are you?" Peter demands. "Why are you here?"

"Ask and it will be given to you; look and you will find."

What follows is a day of fishing unlike any other in Peter's life. Thousands of fish fill his nets. His shoulders burn from the strain of pulling them all into the boat. His nets begin to tear. But Peter casts again and again and again, and every time the nets come back full. Other boats soon set out from the shore as Peter is forced to call for help.

"See?" Andrew says when he arrives. "What did I tell you?"

Peter doesn't answer. He merely studies Jesus and wants to know more about this outrageous individual. As the day ends, too exhausted to steer his boat to shore, Peter collapses atop the pile of fish filling the hold. "How did this happen?" he asks Jesus in a tone of desperation. He can feel a tear welling in his eye. Something in his gut tells him that the direction of his life has just changed.

Jesus does not respond, although he is quite aware that this rough-edged fisherman has just become his first true disciple. It is a beginning of a new world for the both of them.

"Teacher, I am a sinner," Peter tells Jesus. "I am not a seeker, just a mere fisherman."

"So follow me," Jesus finally responds. "And don't be afraid. Follow me and I will make you a fisher of men."

"But what are we going to do?" asks Peter.

"Change the world," Jesus answers.

When Jesus spoke to me, I followed. Others joined us, and soon our numbers grew, and all who heard him felt his power.

CHAPTER TWO

MISSION

The marketplace is crowded. The midday sun beats down hard, and flies alight on the fresh meats hanging in the butcher's stall. One booth over, the wife of a fisherman tries in vain to keep the sun off last night's catch, quietly praying that someone will buy the fish before it spoils. Vegetables, honey, and dates are for sale. The baker is the busiest vendor of all, with crowds lining up to purchase their daily bread, the symbolic reminder of God's ultimate authority over their future. It would be foolish to buy "monthly bread." It would spoil. They buy it day by day, living in the moment, not fixated on a future they cannot control. That gives the people of Israel an important sense of peace at a time when their nation is tormented.

A foreign army still controls the country. People suffer from taxes and the excesses of the Roman rulers. Some days their bodies and spirits are sapped of energy, and they can't remember a time when they weren't drained and beaten down. This simple marketplace of friends and neighbors, and food for sustenance, offers a few moments of peace.

For one woman in the crowd, there is no peace. Her mind has snapped and she is tormented by inner voices. Her face is dirty and contorted from her suffering, and she sweats profusely. She behaves like a mad dog, her eyes wild and mouth snarling. No one makes eye contact with her or offers her help.

A group of Roman soldiers strut into the marketplace and immediately begin to abuse the woman. They steal fruit from a vendor, who is powerless to stop them, then form a circle around the crazed woman and throw fruit at her. The game becomes more fun as she bobs and weaves to avoid their throws.

"Get out of my way!" she screams at the Romans. "Stop spying on me! Stop it—leave me alone!"

After a few moments the Romans grow bored and move on. But another man approaches her, offering help. It is Peter, the newly anointed fisher of men.

"Stop following me! Get out of my way!" she screams, weaving her way through the crowd.

When Peter reaches out to help her, she spits in his face and lunges into the mass of people.

"Leave her!" someone yells to him. "She's possessed by demons. You can't help her."

Peter doesn't give up. He presses through the crowd, right behind the woman. She breaks through into an open space, grabs a pot from a stall, and then hurls it at Peter. She turns to run once again, but finds herself standing face-to-face with Jesus. "What do you want?" she bawls at him, completely unafraid. Her are eyes are clouded with confusion and rage.

When Jesus says nothing, she marches right up to him, raises the broken pot above her head, and stares defiantly into his eyes—imbued with a profound wisdom and peace.

"Come out of her!" Jesus commands the demon.

Violent energy whooshes out of the woman. Her face freezes in shock, her body loses its taut posture, and she collapses. She sobs, her shoulders heaving and torso shaking as the demons leave her, one by one. Her shaking slows. She looks up into Jesus' eyes once again and finds herself transformed by the divine spirit that pours out of him. The woman tries to speak, but she is too overwhelmed to make a sound.

Jesus gently places his hand on her forehead. "I will strengthen you and help you," he tells her.

She smiles. Her mind is clear, as if she has just emerged from a nightmare.

"What is your name?" Jesus asks.

"Mary. Mary of Magdala."

"Come with me, Mary."

Peter watches Jesus approach him. The fisherman shakes his head in wonder. He knows that she has just learned what Peter and the other men who have joined him as disciples of Jesus already know: Jesus embodies God's promise of salvation. But the world has yet to discover who this extraordinary, charismatic man truly is.

Peter studies the faces of others in the crowd. They express wonder at the instant change that has come over the mad-woman Mary. He hears their whispers: "It's him...." "It's that preacher..." "It's the prophet..."

Others are cynical. They've seen it all before. They're suspicious of this quiet carpenter. They don't believe he's a prophet.

The Roman soldiers study Jesus as if he is a threat. Their job, should this be the case, would be to subdue him immediately.

But Jesus doesn't give them cause to do so. His every action is one of peace. "Love one another," he tells his follow-ers. "By this will all men know that you are my disciples, if you love one another."

Word of Jesus' miracles—as some are calling his healing powers—spreads quickly through Galilee. Everywhere he travels, crowds gather. Hundreds flock to his side, shuffling for position in the moving tide of humanity that instantly engulfs Jesus when he enters a town with his disciples.

The phenomenon grows with every mile and every foot-step, every village and town. The disciples do their best to shield Jesus, but people long for a look from those powerful eyes, or merely to touch the hem of his cloak. "Mercy, mercy, Lord have mercy," Peter mumbles again and again as he sees this growing adulation. "Where do they all come from? So much hunger. So much need."

In one small town the scene grows even more bizarre. Knowing that they cannot get to Jesus through the throngs, four young men clamber from roof to roof, carrying another man on a stretcher.

For a practical man like Peter, the decision to follow Jesus brings tests and challenges he never imagined—tests like the one that unfolds when he attempts to get Jesus away from the crowds by drawing him into a small empty house for a few moments of peace. No sooner do they enter the home than Peter hears the sounds of roof tiles breaking, and those four young men dragging their paralyzed father to a perch on the roof.

Peter goes outside to wave them away, but the men pretend not to hear him. They punch a hole in the thatch roof. Daylight appears in the room. From inside the open doorway, silhouetted against the mass of sunlit followers outside, Jesus begins to speak to the crowd outside. "Come to me, all you who are weary and burdened, and I will give you rest.

"Take my yoke upon you and learn from me," he continues, even as Peter tries in vain to keep the intruders out of their house. But it's too late. One young man has already dropped into the room, and his father has been lowered into his arms. Even if Peter had the power to reverse this situation, there's no going back.

"For I am gentle and humble in heart," Jesus continues, "and you will find rest for your souls."

Only now does Jesus acknowledge the ruckus behind him. He turns to see the paralyzed man lying on the floor, surrounded by Peter and the man's four sons.

Jesus walks toward the man. Peter stands back to make room. The paralyzed man cannot walk, but he can move his arms. He reaches up his fingers to touch Jesus.

Jesus does not extend his arms to the man. Instead, he slowly pulls his hand away. As he does so, the paralyzed man, so desperate to touch Jesus, reaches out farther and farther—and the more he reaches, the more Jesus pulls back.

The look on Jesus' face is one of complete calm. He sees the struggle in the eyes of the man, a struggle that he quietly encourages. Finally, Jesus touches his fingertips to those of the paralyzed man. "Your sins are forgiven."

Mary Magdalene, who has followed Jesus along with the disciples, knows firsthand what Jesus can accomplish. She thought she had seen everything, but her mouth opens wide in shock at what is taking place.

The man realizes he is no longer lying down, unable to move. He is sitting completely upright. Jesus says nothing. The man is emboldened and tries to stand. Everyone in the village knows this is impossible; he has been completely handicapped for years—his sons have had to care for him around the clock. His eyes fixed on Jesus, the man stands.

The crowd closest to the doorway backs away in shock. Those farther back press forward to see what has happened. Heads crane upward to get a better look. Some close their eyes in prayer.

The once-paralyzed man is swept away in euphoria. He hops and jumps like a child, dazzled. These simple movements soon become an impromptu dance, and his sons soon join in. The disciples dance, too. Hands start clapping in the small room, and soon the crowd outside joins in. Men start singing as the crowd sways to the beat of this unlikely and profound miracle. They know that this proves Jesus' real connection to the power of God.

The healed man is exhausted. He stops dancing and comes to Jesus, who softly places his hand on the man's forehead. "Go home now, friend," Jesus tells him. "Your sins are forgiven."

These are not the words the man expected to hear. He shuffles his feet and looks at the ground. His friends stop dancing, the smiles gone from their faces. Soon, the entire crowd has gone silent. Jesus' words could be viewed as an act of blasphemy. Only God can forgive sins. To condone his words would be to act against God's authority.

Those in the crowd who belong to the religious sect known as the Pharisees understand that Jesus' words are more significant than his casting out demons or healing broken bodies. Devoted students of God's law, they distinguish between the powers God assigns to men and those He keeps for Himself. Pharisees listen to every teacher in Israel, paying close attention to their words for signs of either truth or blasphemy. No man equals Jesus. The claims he makes and the command with which he speaks is unsurpassed. The masses have never rallied around a teacher so quickly and with such enthusiasm. Jesus knows what the Pharisees are thinking in their hearts.

One of the Pharisees speaks up. "You can't do that."

"Do what?" Jesus asks.

"Forgive."

Jesus looks at him. Then he looks at the man he has just healed.

Peter leans over and whispers to Jesus, "Don't these people understand what you just did?"

Jesus looks calmly upon Peter. For the world to understand his mission, Jesus must begin by making those closest to him understand. "Which is easier to say: 'Your sins are forgiven,' or 'Take up your bed and walk'?" he asks rhetorically.

The leader of the Pharisees, a man named Simon, shakes his head in disgust and leads his men away. He knows Jesus has become someone to follow very closely. They will deal with him some other day.

"Come on," Jesus tells his disciples. He leads them out the door and into the crowd, in the opposite direction from the

Pharisees. "Our work here is done. We have a long way to go. We'd better get moving." Then he turns and begins walking out of town, leaving the people of the village to wonder what exactly they just witnessed.

———

Jesus' disciples have chosen to be brothers and sisters in Christ. Though they may not yet realize it, this puts them in the vanguard of a revolution—a religious revolution, one not found in ancient texts or in Jewish oral history. Rather, it is a new promise that connects God's will to people's daily lives. This is a difficult concept to grasp, but if the disciples are ever to lead, they need training.

Jesus takes the time to teach his disciples during their daily walks from city to city. His simple, poetic words are delivered casually and gently. Jesus prefers to explain a difficult concept over time, never talking down to his followers, patiently letting the words soak in until they understand them fully.

But Jesus doesn't just preach to the disciples. His revolution is a grassroots movement: he preaches on dirt roads, in fields and villages, to farmers and fishermen and all manner of travelers. These working-class people of Israel form the backbone of his growing ministry. He stops often, standing on a hillside or by a river to address the thousands who flock to hear him, and preaches his new vision for the relationship between God and man. His goal is to liberate these oppressed people, who suffer so dearly under the Roman tax burden. But Jesus has no plans to form an army to save the Israelites from Rome. He wants to free them from something far more dire: sin.

Many don't understand. When Jesus says, "Blessed are they who hunger for righteousness, for they shall be filled," it sounds like a call to arms against Rome.

But then he says things like, "Blessed are the peacemakers, for they shall be called Sons of God."

While many in the crowds hear his words as those of a political radical, many more are coming to understand Jesus' message of love. One evening, he stands on a rocky hillside as the sun sets. He has chosen this moment because his audience of farmers, shepherds, laborers, and their families do not have the financial luxury of taking time away from their occupation during working hours. They stand before Jesus, their long day finished, hands and arms sore from backbreaking labor, and listen to his words. They experience peace washing over their bodies, minds, and hearts. His loving presence touches them.

The evening sun is a dull orange, and the crowd is silent as Jesus tells them about his Father. He teaches the people how to pray, and even what words to say: "Our Father," Jesus begins, "who is in heaven, hallowed be thy name."

Jesus prompts them to really think about what this new prayer says. It begins by praising God's name. It continues with a plea for their daily bread, so that their bellies will be full. Then it turns to a request for forgiveness, because sin will keep them out of heaven. "Forgive us our trespasses," Jesus says, "as we forgive those who trespass against us."

He continues, and the crowd goes right along with him, memorizing the words so that they may say them in their own time of prayer. "Lead us not into temptation, but deliver us from evil."

So there it is. This is the new way to pray: Praise God. Depend upon him for your daily needs. Ask forgiveness. Forgive others. Ask God to keep you from trouble, and the pain that comes with sin.

The people know they can pray like this. But it all seems so...easy. Where is the animal sacrifice? Where is the need for a grand Temple, since they can say this prayer anywhere, and at any time?

The sun is almost set by the time Jesus is finished. His audience presses forward to touch him. Their souls have been renewed by this new approach to prayer and God. They are strengthened, encouraged, and comforted. They go back to their homes, brimming with new hope for their future, thanks to Jesus' insistence that God has prepared a place in heaven for all of them. This life of toil and strife and Roman oppression will end someday, but the peace and love of heaven will be forever. To the people of Galilee, Jesus' words feel like a spiritual rebirth.

To the Pharisees, they sound dangerous.

It is daytime, in a small town in Galilee. Hundreds of Israelites wait in line for the mandatory audience with the taxman to pay their tribute. The sound of coins being dropped onto the counting tables fills the air.

The first portion of these monies go to Rome. That much is decreed by law. Failure to pay can mean imprisonment or death. But Rome has long had trouble collecting taxes, so they have farmed out the work to a group of freelance collectors. These men are all Jews, just like the people lined up to pay. So what they're doing is an act of extortion against their own people. For to impose additional fees upon the burden that the already overwhelmed Israelis are suffering is not just onerous, it is treason. The covenant between God and Abraham does not exist between these cruel men and the people they extort. Those who gather taxes are thought worthy of nothing but contempt.

Jesus and his disciples now pass by the lines of sullen men who wait to pay their taxes. "Collaborators and traitors. Taking money from their own people. Sinners all," Peter grumbles beneath his breath. Criticizing the tax collectors is the same as criticizing Rome. He could pay for this indiscretion with his life.

The disciples are stunned to see Jesus carefully scrutinizing one of the tax collectors, whose hands count coins more slowly, his eyes, unwilling to look directly at his victims, betray sadness and doubt. The man's name, the disciples are soon to learn, is Levi. Despite appearing soft or even supportive to his fellow Jews, he is a taxman nonetheless.

"What do you see, Lord?" asks the disciple named John—not John the Baptist, who is still interred in the grisly jails of Herod Antipas.

Jesus doesn't answer. So John tries to see Levi through the eyes of Jesus. What he sees is the look of a man lost in sin, longing for a way out but not believing that such a path exists. Jesus' gaze has been so hard and so direct that soon Levi raises his head to stare back at this powerful energy he feels. His eyes soon connect with those of Jesus, just as the Son of God issues the following order: "Follow me."

In the blink of an eye, Levi understands the summons. "Follow me" is the same as saying, "Believe in me." Free from sin and doubt and worry and faithlessness. *No matter what else happens in my life, I am free to choose.* The moment Levi places his faith in Jesus and follows him, his sins are forgiven and he is free. Levi stands up and walks away from the table, leaving piles of uncounted coins in his wake. The clink of coins from the other tax collectors goes on undiminished until they see what Levi has done. Struck dumb, they stop their work and stare openmouthed at the utter stupidity of Levi walking away from a life of wealth and ease . . . and for what? To follow this revolutionary named Jesus?

The disciples are incensed. Peter glares at Jesus, enraged that the new disciple is the lowest form of life known to the people of Israel.

"You don't like that I talk to tax collectors and sinners," Jesus says to Peter. "But search your heart and hear what I have to say: It's not the healthy who need a doctor, but the sick. I'm not here to call the righteous. I'm here for the sinners."

Peter has no response. His name means "Rock," and it fits. He is as sturdy and hard as the day is long. His hands are calloused and his ways are not always polite. Following Jesus is a huge gamble, meaning the loss of income during those times when they are not out fishing. Levi becomes a disciple, and will from now on be called Matthew. Like it or not, Peter is loyal to Jesus and follows him to the next town on their journey.

Jesus squats in the town square, drawing in the dust with his finger. He is not drawing a picture, but a series of letters. He is not alone, nor is the scene tranquil. Directly behind him, a crowd is gathering to watch a stoning. A woman is forced to stand in front of a high wall, facing this crowd. Between the woman and the crowd rises a pile of smooth large stones. When the time comes, each man in the group will be asked to lift a stone and throw it hard at her face. They will do this again and again until she is unconscious, and then keep throwing stones until she is dead—or the pile is depleted, whichever comes first. Death always comes before the pile is used up.

The Pharisees have seen Jesus' popularity grow and watched with dismay as their own followers have taken up with him. They firmly believe that he is a blasphemer, and they have been searching for a way to prevent their entire populace from following him.

At one of his sermons, Jesus quite clearly told the crowd to uphold the law, knowing that to ignore Roman law would mean a wave of punishment against his new followers. In Israel, Roman law and religious law are closely intertwined. If the Pharisees can catch Jesus in the act of breaking a religious law, then they can try him before a religious court. Based on the words of the Pharisees, if Jesus is also shown to be a radical or a revolutionary whose teachings will incite rebellion against Rome, he could also be tried before a Roman tribunal. But there is absolutely no evidence that Jesus has committed a crime nor broken the Law of Moses. A test is their last refuge.

The young woman standing before the wall has been accused of adultery. She is an outcast in the local society. Absolutely no man or woman will stand and come to her defense. Her guilt is assumed. Her fate is sealed.

The men in the crowd grasp their stones, eager to throw. The disciples and Mary Magdalene stand to one side, with Mary holding the condemned woman's sobbing infant daughter. The Pharisees lord over the proceedings, eager to spring their trap.

Jesus, meanwhile, scribbles in the dirt.

Simon the Pharisee steps before the crowd. He is grand-standing, making a very public point. So when he speaks, it is not to the terrified woman standing behind him. His focus is on Jesus, always Jesus, even as the man from Naza-reth continues on dragging his forefinger through the dust. "Teacher," he says to Jesus, "this woman was caught in the act of adultery. In the Law, Moses commanded us to stone this woman. Now what do you say?" He is using the question as trap, looking for a basis to accuse him.

Jesus ignores Simon.

The disciples cry out to Jesus: "Please, say something to help her."

Then, to the shock of all who watch, Jesus reaches down and selects a fine throwing stone from the pile. Mary's face shows utter bewilderment, and there is a mild gasp from those who are gathered. Jesus walks over and lines up next to the Pharisees, each of whom now hold a stone, facing the condemned woman.

Now the Pharisees and each of the men so eager to draw blood see the words Jesus has written: JUDGE NOT, LEST YOU BE JUDGED.

As they stare at the words, letting them rest upon their hearts, Jesus strolls back and forth in front of the throwing line. He holds his rock up in his hand for all to see as he scrutinizes the rocks held by the others. "Let the man who is without sin throw the first stone." Jesus offers his rock to each man, even as his eyes challenge them all with the utter certainty that they have all sinned.

Even the Pharisees cannot look Jesus in the eye.

Jesus walks over to the woman. His back is to the throwing line, leaving him vulnerable to attack. Just one angry throw could end his life. "Have they thrown anything?" Jesus asks the woman, his voice thick with mercy and grace. Behind he hears the dull thuds of rocks hitting the earth. But the rocks are being dropped, not thrown. All the men turn silently and walks quickly to their homes as their own sins—theft, adultery, and much more—nag at their consciences.

"Go," Jesus tells the woman. "Go and sin no more."

She doesn't need to be told twice. Breaking past him in a second, she grabs her baby from Mary's arms and runs quickly into the distance.

Simon the Pharisee looks angrily at Jesus. But there is no stone in his hand.

"I desire mercy," Jesus explains to him with his palms upraised, "not sacrifice."

But Simon is not done with him. Jesus has saved a sinner, but the chances of his reconciling his differences with the Pharisees recede with every sinner that he saves. Unless they do, however, Jesus is sure to come out the loser. The Pharisees are politically connected and powerful. One day they will set a trap for Jesus that he won't escape.

———

The Pharisees now focus on ensnaring him in a debate about the scriptures—theological ambush. Two things the Pharisees don't realize: their trap could catch either side; and as a devout Jew, Jesus knows scripture better than anyone. The Pharisees now begin to follow Jesus, watching his every move. They even invite him to break bread with them, on the pretense that both sides can talk and get to know one another better.

Jesus and two of his disciples dine with the Pharisees inside a small room at Simon's home. Jesus sits by the door, listening as Simon expounds on his latest religious theories. On the other side of the table sit a small group of Pharisees. Their faces are a study in rapt attention as they give Simon their complete respect.

Mary Magdalene slips quietly into the room, doing her best

to be unobtrusive. The last thing she wants to do is interrupt Simon or to become the center of attention. But that's precisely what she does, for Mary is not alone. She leads a young woman, who is a sinner, into the room. The woman carries a small stone jar. Its contents are a gift for Jesus, and her eyes instantly seek him out in the soft light of the room.

When Simon sees the woman with Mary, he thunders, "You have no business here! Go and offer your body elsewhere!"

Utterly humiliated, the woman moves toward the door. She desperately wants to leave. Her shame is complete. But before she can leave, Jesus reaches out a hand and gently touches her arm. She stops. "Please," Jesus tells her. "Do what you have come here to do."

The words of Jesus give her courage to endure the torment of social scorn. What she planned to do won't take long. She will get it done and then hurry off. Kneeling in front of Jesus, she removes his sandals. A tear falls onto his bare, dirty feet. She uncovers her long dark hair and wipes her tear away with it. Then, hands shaking, she reaches for the small jar and unstops the lid. The scent of perfume, fragrant and delicate, blossoms in the air. The woman pours a few drops of the precious liquid on Jesus' feet, and rubs it in with her bare hands.

Simon can barely believe what he is seeing. His first instinct is to throw these heretics from his home, but then he realizes that this is the perfect moment to lecture Jesus on his impudence. "They say you are a prophet," Simon sneers. "Your friends certainly treat you like one. Well, let me tell you this: if you were a real prophet, you would never let a woman such as this touch you."

Jesus doesn't respond. He has been moved by the woman's kindness and humble servitude, and he knows that this moment means everything to her.

Simon continues: "Look at her. She's a sinner!"

Jesus gently lays his hand atop her head. "Whatever sins she has committed, she is forgiven."

Simon puffs himself up and points a long finger at Jesus. "This is my house. Do you understand? And in my house what matters is God's law. We are devoted to it."

Jesus smiles at Simon and turns back to the woman. "Thank you," he says as she picks up her jar and leaves. The woman is consumed with joy and a sense of peace, but just as eager to flee from Simon and his angry tirade about her character.

"Cursed is anyone who does not uphold the law," blusters Simon, but now his words are intended for Jesus. "To this," he concludes, "all people should say, 'Amen.'"

Incense rises in a thin wisp, spreading its sickly sweet aroma slowly over the dimly lit interior of the synagogue. The congregation bow their heads in attendant worship as Simon stands before them, teaching. The Torah rests before him, and his fingers slide slowly across each line as he reads.

Simon is at peace in his synagogue. It is more than just the meeting place where he can preach to the community, but also a spiritual home. A place where he can lead his followers in devotion to the law—a gift from God. That tranquility is interrupted as Jesus and his disciples step through the door. Simon keeps teaching, even as he carefully tracks Jesus' movement toward the congregation. The bearded carpenter seeks out a man with a withered hand, and leans close to have a word with him.

Peter, always pragmatic, moans to himself, for he knows what is coming. "Surely," he mumbles, "he wouldn't dare. Not here. Not today."

This is the Sabbath, a time God has prescribed for rest and spiritual reflection. Absolutely no work or other exertion can take place on this holy day. Peter looks toward Simon, the Pharisee, who is staring at Jesus. The synagogue has grown silent. All teaching has stopped. All are eyes on Jesus and the man with the deformed hand.

"Today is the Sabbath," Jesus says to no one in particular, though his words are quite clearly aimed at Simon and the Pharisees. "Tell me: is it lawful to do good or to do harm on the Sabbath—to save a life or to kill?"

Simon's face is beet red. His eyes bore into Jesus. "Neither," Simon says under his breath.

Jesus asks the man to stand. Slowly, the man rises. He looks uncertain and self-conscious.

"Most of you have sheep," Jesus says to the congregation. "If on your way here, you saw that one had fallen into a ditch, would you not reach down and pull it out?"

He then takes the man's hand in full view of the entire room. "Then is this man worth less than a sheep?"

The crowd gasps as the man's hand is no longer a withered claw. Instead, he is completely healed. His work done, Jesus immediately turns and heads for the door.

"How dare you!" Simon roars, grasping hold of his robe with two hands and ripping it open in full view of the congregation. The Pharisees standing nearby do the same, making it clear that they have seen something unclean and wish God's forgiveness.

Jesus doesn't see any of this. Only Peter who realizes he's been left behind and races to catch up.

Simon isn't far behind. Enraged by Jesus' behavior, he races into the street and grabs the healed man's hand. He jerks the man to a halt and then raises the new hand into the air. There is no escaping Simon's grip, particularly when other Pharisees come to gather around, so the man is soon paraded through the streets like a trophy. He is evidence to one and all that Jesus has violated the scripture.

Or worse. "This healing is the work of demons," screeches Simon.

Those standing nearby are in awe. They have known this man their whole lives. How is it possible that his hand is completely healed? This is a source of wonder, not shame.

Simon ignores their looks and pleads his case. He knows his audience.

"He's never studied the law, but he's happy to break it," adds Simon.

Despite their amazement about the healing, the crowd is now aghast.

Simon presses on. "He recruits tax collectors and sinful women to do his bidding. He defiles God's law, and His synagogue—your synagogue."

The crowd becomes agitated and unruly. It begins to feel dangerous. Jesus is unruffled and as calm as ever. "Love your enemies," he cautions Peter. "Love those who persecute you."

"We're just supposed to take it?" Peter asks incredulously.

Jesus, the disciples, and Mary Magdalene battle their way through the mob. The city's streets are now in a state of unrest. Roman soldiers wade into the fracas, grabbing the Pharisees and dragging them back toward the synagogue. The Romans are only too happy to mete out punishment with fists and clubs. Jesus goes one way, leading his followers to safety. The Pharisees go another. In the streets, it escalates into a bloody scuffle between the oppressed Jews and the Roman legionnaires. Afterward, as tensions continues to mount, the Pharisees plot how they might kill Jesus.

Jesus has no intention of waging a battle for religious power. But as his ministry grows, he finds himself wading into a complex quagmire of political and religious movements. God, Rome, and religion are intertwined throughout Israel, and two rival factions fight for control. Accepting only the written word of Moses as law and rejecting all other subsequent revelations, the Sadducees think of themselves as the Old Believers. The Pharisees additionally believe in the resurrection of the dead, as well as an afterlife of either heavenly rewards or eternal damnation, taking the Mosaic tradition and the remainder of the Torah as their authoritative text. Politically the Sadducees are a stronger, more powerful force. They represent the priestly aristocracy and the power structure of Israel. Their religious duties are focused on the Temple. The Pharisees represent the common man. The Sadducees view worship in the Temple as the main focus of the law.

The most powerfully religious in Israel make up the Sanhedrin. This council is the supreme court for all Jewish disputes, and it even has the power to hand down death sentences. Despite the Sanhedrin's power, the Romans are still their masters. It is led by a high priest appointed by the

Romans, and Rome can just as easily remove him. Caiaphas, the middle-aged high priest, is in the awkward position of balancing the material demands of his Roman masters with the spiritual demands of the Jewish people.

At the moment, Caiaphas is faced with an even greater dilemma. Military banners bearing the Roman eagle have been hung overnight in the great Temple. They brazenly and publicly flaunt God's ban on the use of idolatrous images in the Temple's precinct. All Jews know this is an invasion of their sacred place.

What is Caiaphas to do? If he makes a stand against the Romans he will be stripped of his power. If he does not, his own people will see him as a puppet and a figurehead—a man who pretends to have power but lacks authority. He knows he must make a stand, and to only one man—Pontius Pilate.

Since the breakup of Israel following the death of Herod the Great, Roman prefects have governed the province of Judea. In Rome, Judea is seen as nothing more than the graveyard of ambition. Four prefects have come and gone within twenty years. Pilate is the latest to attempt to control this fractious, troubled backwater. Feeling the need to make a name for himself and stamp his authority on the region, Pilate has moved a new squadron of troops to Jerusalem. As is common practice within the Roman Empire, the arrival of a new group of soldiers also means the arrival of their unit's standard. Hence the eagle banners.

Caiaphas is afraid of Pilate, and with good reason: the new prefect is known for his tough demeanor. He has no trouble oppressing the Jewish people, for he believes the full force of Roman power is sometimes necessary to keep the peace.

But the longer Caiaphas delays his confrontation with Pilate, the more dire the situation becomes. Word of the idolatrous banners, and of the defiling of the Temple, spreads like wildfire throughout Judea. Thousands soon gather in the main square of Caesarea, Pilate's home, to protest.

Caesarea is fifty miles from Jerusalem, on a coastal plain caressed each day by cool Mediterranean breezes. It is the hub of Rome's government in Judea, built by Herod the Great but now the home of Pontius Pilate. He can live anywhere in Israel he wants, but Pilate prefers the tranquility of Caesarea and smell of those ocean breezes to the crowded, manic pace of Jerusalem.

Pilate looks down on the mob from his marbled residence. His well-muscled chest is bare and covered in sweat. As a Roman soldier himself, Pilate knows the value of physical conditioning, and he's spent the last hour sparring with wooden practice swords. Though smaller than a war sword, they are just as heavy, and Pilate can feel the heaviness in his forearms and shoulders from the exertion.

An aide hands Pilate a tunic. Outside, the crowd's roaring and chanting is deafening, as if they have the privilege of saying and doing anything they like without punishment.

Perhaps they are unaware that the Roman Empire operates through a mix of enlightened self-interest and overwhelming force. Pilate must put an end to this. He wraps the tunic around his chest and steps into the window so that the crowd can see him. In an instant, the noise stops. Pilate turns to his aide. "Have the men seal the square. Immediately."

"Yes, sir," says the aide, rushing off to deliver the order.

The crowd gazes up at their prefect, waiting for him to speak. But Pilate says nothing, preferring to watch the lines of soldiers assembling in the streets just off the square. A second group of soldiers is now working its way into the front of the crowd, separating the leaders of the protest from the rest.

Only then does Pilate speak: "Go home. In the name of the Emperor, I order you to go home. Leave now and no harm will come to you."

The crowd is still.

Up front, its leaders kneel.

The officer in charge of the soldiers glances up to Pilate for instruction. Pilate responds with a simple nod of his head.

The officer draws his sword, and his men immediately do the same.

The leaders of the protest, still on their knees, pull their robes off their shoulders to expose their necks. They are willing to be beheaded.

Roman intimidation relies upon fear. The soldiers are clearly uncomfortable slaughtering these protesters. Word of this will get back to Rome, if he murders this crowd. It will reflect poorly on his job performance, for Pilate has been sent to govern the Jews, not butcher them.

He steps back from the window, knowing that today the Jews have gotten the best of him. Pilate tastes the bile of humiliation in his throat, and longs to run out into the crowd and run a sword through each of those protesters. Even better, he should have them crucified. That's how the Romans deal with troublemakers: nail them to the cross. Maybe next time. Pilate retreats into the privacy of his home and orders the removal of all banners from the temple.

Far out in the countryside, miles from Caesarea and the Mediterranean, Jesus and his disciples clean up after their afternoon meal. They lounge next to a stream, enjoying the warmth of the sun on their faces and the tickle of fresh green grass against their bare feet. It is a wondrous day, and despite their meager possessions and the possibility of yet another run-in with the Pharisees when they get to the next town, they revel in these simple pleasures.

Peter spies a young man approaching the group. He bears an offering of fruit. The man's clothes mark him as a city boy—too bright, too new, not rugged enough for long days in the fields or on a fishing boat.

But they have no reason to doubt his sincerity, so Matthew gratefully accepts the fruit and leads the young man to Jesus.

"I'd like to learn from you," the young man stammers. "To follow you, if you will let me. And to serve in any way that I can."

Jesus has already shouldered his bag and is beginning to move on down the road. But he invites the young man to walk with him.

Peter eyes the man with suspicion. "We went through all sorts of trials to become disciples," he mutters to Matthew. "Now this guy just walks in from who knows where and gets to join?"

Jesus calls Matthew, former tax collector and professional bookkeeper, to walk with him and the new disciple. With just a few words and the transfer of a money bag from Matthew's hand into those of the stranger, Jesus makes the new disciple the group treasurer.

Peter is outraged. His instinct is to rely on logic, not faith. But what Jesus has done is clearly an act of reckless and rather spontaneous faith.

"What's his name?" Peter asks Andrew.

"Judas," he answers. "Judas Iscariot."

It's dusk as Jesus and the disciples walk up a long hill that leads to the next town. Children run to greet them, but otherwise it appears that they are in for an ordinary evening. They'll find a place to sleep and get a meal. Perhaps Jesus will teach, or maybe he won't. All in all, they're just glad to be sleeping with a roof over their heads after many a night sleeping outdoors.

But as Jesus leads the way up and over the top of the hill, the apostles gasp in shock. Thousands upon thousands of people fill the valley below. They stand on the shores of a silvery sea, waiting anxiously to hear the words of Jesus.

The instant the crowds catch sight of him, they rush up the hillside, all trying to get a spot in front when Jesus begins teaching.

"Would you look at all those people?" gasps Peter.

"Yes," Jesus answers. "How are we going to feed them all?"

"Do what?"

"Feed them. It's late. I don't see any cooking fires. They must be famished," Jesus replies.

Judas, trying to show his practical nature, shakes the money bag, and a small handful of coins clank inside. "You'll need a bit more than this," he tells Jesus.

Peter shoots Judas a look.

"Go out into the crowd," Jesus tells his disciples. "And bring back as much food as you can."

They come back with almost nothing: five loaves of bread and two fish. There's not enough to feed the disciples themselves, let alone roughly five thousand. The crowd consumed the contents of their food baskets hours ago, as they waited patiently for Jesus. Now those baskets are quite empty.

Jesus seems unbothered. "Thank You, Father," he prays over the little food they have gathered. "Thank You for what You bring us."

The disciples begin to distribute the food, and the empty baskets overflow with bread and fish—so much that the crowd has seconds, and then thirds.

Peter, that practical man, is once again humbled by Jesus' greatness. As he watches the people eat, he remembers his own miraculous first meeting with Jesus, and how his boat soon groaned from the weight of all that fish.

Jesus comes to Peter and looks him in the eye. There is a loving warmth in Jesus' gaze, once again reminding Peter to let go of his practical nature to put all his trust in God.

The crowd is soon demanding more food, and clamoring to proclaim Jesus as the new King of the Jews. But he sends them away, knowing that the miracle they observed will be more than enough to fortify their faith for some time to come.

In the morning, when it comes time to sail across the sea to their next destination, Jesus is nowhere to be seen. He has told them to go to the far side without him, so that he can go alone into the mountains and pray. Led by Peter, the disciples take their boat and begin the long sail across the vast sea. The small boat is packed to the gunwales with disciples and their small bags of belongings. Peter is the man of the sea, so he commands the helm. His eyes scan the darkening sky anxiously, for he knows a coming storm when he sees one. The wind blows hard and cold. Waves smash against the hull, forcing the small boat to pitch wildly.

"Where are you?" Peter mutters as sea spray covers his face. His eyes scan the horizon, brows knitted into a frown. The weather is only getting worse. The gusts have grown to gale force, making it almost impossible for Peter to look forward into the wind. He has reefed the small sail to ensure that the boat won't capsize, but that also means the boat can't be steered. The disciples row furiously, and Peter has one hand on the tiller, but it's no use: the tiny boat bobs like a cork atop the furious seas, as directionless as a sinner who doesn't know God.

"Oh, mercy," Peter moans. "Why did we leave without Jesus? He would know what to do." Lightning flashes. In the distance, he sees a solitary figure. *Perhaps we're closer to land than I thought*, Peter says to himself, staring into the blackness. Another bolt of lightning. And again, Peter sees a man standing straight ahead, although much closer this time. Peter squints his eyes to see what's out there and feels the wind blast his face. If this man is standing on a dock, Peter should keep a sharp eye, otherwise the boat will be smashed on the rocks.

A new bolt of lightning is followed immediately by another. Peter is blinded by the light, but forces himself to search for this mystery man. Peter gasps. He has seen Jesus. Peter is sure of it. He tries to stand up in the boat, but it's like standing on the bare back of a bucking mule. The other disciples have seen Jesus in the darkness and also try to stand for a better look. "Sit down," Peter orders.

His eyes peer into the darkness for Jesus. "Teacher," he cries out, his words almost swallowed by the wind. "Talk to me!"

And just like that, he can clearly see Jesus standing atop the waves. That's right: standing on the water. Peter knows that he's not hallucinating. What other man can do such a thing? Is Jesus merely a man? Peter thinks of all the times that Jesus made mention of "my Father," as if God were truly his parent. But maybe it's all true. Could it be? In the depths of his heart, Peter finds a new kernel of faith. He tries to wrap his mind around this novel concept that Jesus is who he says he is: the Son of God. Not just a charismatic teacher. Not just a prophet. But the one and only Son of God.

"It's a ghost," Thomas, one of the disciples, cries out in terror.

Peter stills his troubled thoughts. "Lord," he shouts, "if it is you, tell me to come to you on the water."

"Come to me, Peter."

Peter has two hands on the gunwales and vaults himself

up and over the side. He is not drenched by waves or gasping for breath in the water. He is standing. A terrified smile flashes across Peter's face at the absurdity of it all. He laughs, a great belly laugh in the middle of the all-consuming storm, and walks confidently toward Jesus, his eyes locked on his teacher's. His heart swells with newfound faith, and Peter knows that he will never look upon Jesus the same way again. *The Son of God*, Peter thinks. *I am looking into the eyes of the man who is truly the Son of God.*

Suddenly, the practical side of his mind tells him it is impossible to walk on water. He looks down into the depths, and the one thing that has led him to follow Jesus all this while—his faith—suddenly disappears. Peter sinks. His robes weigh him down, and he plunges farther under the water. He keeps his mouth closed, desperate not to feel water rushing into his lungs, but his chest feels like it will explode from lack of breath. Then Peter feels Jesus pulling his hand, lifting him from the water. In an instant he is out of the waves and lying on the pitching deck, soaking wet. Peter opens his eyes to see a loving Jesus standing over him, his face filled with kindness.

"Peter," he says. "Oh, you of little faith. Why did you doubt?"

Peter is now a changed man, and he desperately wants Jesus to know it. "I have faith, in you. You are my Lord."

Then Jesus calms the storm. He orders the wind to stop,

and to the waves he says, "Be still." At his command, the wind dies down, and all is still. The disciples look at him with the same reverence Peter displayed. "Truly you are the Son of God," they say, bowing down in worship.

———

The sight of Jesus appearing in the middle of the storm, and then walking upon the waves, is not quickly forgotten. Upon reaching the shore, the disciples sit on a hillside, watching the sun rise over the Sea of Galilee, and they cannot stop recounting their individual memories of what they saw. Jesus has set himself apart from them once again, praying alone within sight of their camp. From their lofty perch, they can see from one side to the other of this once tempestuous inland body of water and marvel that it is now as placid as a village well. Their cooking fire is small, for there is little wood in these parts. Peter is still drenched, so he sits as close as he can to the heat in order to dry himself.

John sits beside Peter, who is obviously distraught.

"I let him down," Peter tells John. "I let you all down. I'm sorry."

"No, that was just a moment—a moment we could have never been prepared for."

"Do you think it was a test?"

"I think that this is all a journey, Peter. You can't get there in one step."

Peter laughs. "Where is 'there'?"

It's a rhetorical question, for they both know Peter is alluding to the Promised Land. John looks off to where Jesus is praying. His is a different kind of Promised Land, one not of this earth. John quietly marvels at their teacher's immense powers of concentration.

Jesus' eyes open. He looks directly at John. It's as if he's looking straight into his soul. In that instant, John is reassured. He knows that Jesus is truly the King of the Jews, sent by God to save Israel, but not from the Romans.

———

Rivers of blood flow through the gutters of Jerusalem. The high priest Caiaphas watches over the cleanup of this crimson tide, his face a mask of concern and his heart full of grief. Pilate has had his revenge on the Jews for their riot in Caesarea. When a new aqueduct needed funding, Pilate had requisitioned the Temple coffers. The people of Jerusalem rebelled, and this time Pilate did not turn the other cheek. Hundreds of Jews were put to the sword. Caiaphas is powerless to stop the Roman oppression.

In his ornate palace in Caesarea, Pilate revels in his triumph. The marble floors gleam as the Mediterranean sun shines in through the large windows. Herod built this palace, but to Pilate it's as if the place was designed with his own personal needs in mind. Far from the fanatics of Jerusalem, close to a port from which he can embark for Rome on a moment's notice, and most of all, a bastion of civility in this wretched post with its quarrelsome population. Some days he can even pretend that he's back in Rome.

Pilate sits at his desk as a scribe brings him a stack of official documents. As he signs them, Pilate congratulates himself on how well he handled this latest Jewish rebellion. He knows his behavior will be carefully scrutinized in Rome, and he is certain he had more than enough justification for his brutal response. In his official report, he will honestly tell Emperor Tiberius his no-nonsense approach to the Judean troublemakers is working.

Pilate's signet ring comes down hard on a pool of wax, sealing his official report. If it's rebellion the Jews want, it's suppression that they'll get.

In these these harsh times, it becomes obvious to many Jews that they cannot put their faith in Caiaphas and the Sanhedrin, the Pharisees, or any others of the Jewish religious hierarchy. All eyes focus on Jesus. Some even say that he has power over life itself. He has restored sight to the blind, cured the lame, cast out demons, healed the handicapped, and raised the dead. Some say that if a person has enough faith in Jesus and his teachings, the sick can be healed, the physical body can be made whole, and life itself can be restored.

Caiaphas can't make that claim. Nor can the Pharisees.

Jesus is soon put to the test, as he and his disciples walk through a village, enjoying the games played by the young children and the generally festive atmosphere of the day. A messenger comes running with a desperate plea. He tells Jesus that his friend Lazarus, who lives in a neighboring town, lies dangerously ill. Mary, the woman who anointed Jesus' feet in the home of Simon, and her sister Martha had given up hope until they heard that Jesus was nearby. They see this as a sign from God. They know Jesus can save their brother, and they ask him to come quickly and help them in their hour of need.

Jesus knows her brother Lazarus well. Yet he does nothing. Lazarus lives in a region of Judea whose people had tried to stone Jesus and the disciples. They would risk their lives returning there. The disciples assume this risk must be on Jesus' mind, although it is not like Jesus to back down from a challenge. "Aren't we going to see Lazarus?" they ask him.

"This sickness will not end in death," Jesus tells them. "No, it is for God's glory, so that God's son may be glorified through it."

Two days pass. Finally, Jesus tells the disciples, "Our friend Lazarus has fallen asleep, but I am going there to wake him up."

The disciples are unclear of his meaning. "Lord," they tell him, "if he sleeps he will get better."

"Lazarus is dead," he says bluntly, forced to spell it out to them. "And for your sake I am glad I was not there, so that you may believe. Let us go to him."

"Let us go so that we may die with him," Thomas says glumly, thinking of the Judeans' previous attempt to stone them.

Some days later, Jesus and his disciples make the short walk to Lazarus' village. They find a town consumed in grief. "Are you coming for show?" Mary cries at him through her tears. "You could have saved him."

Jesus says nothing as he keeps on walking toward Lazarus' home.

"We believed in you! We trusted you!" Mary sobs. "You're the healer. You could have saved him. Why didn't you come? Why? Tell me."

Martha, bereft, simply moans when she sees Jesus.

An angry crowd of mourners soon surrounds Jesus and his disciples. The mood is hostile. "Fool," says an unidentified voice in the crowd. "If you were so powerful you should have saved Lazarus from dying." The disciples stiffen.

"I am the resurrection and the life," Jesus tells Martha and Mary. "If anyone believes in me, he will live, even though he dies. And whoever lives and believes in me will never die. Do you believe this?"

"Yes, Lord. I believe that you are the Christ, the Son of

God who was to come into the world." Mary weeps as she speaks, and Jesus is deeply moved.

"Where have you laid him?" Jesus asks. By now Lazarus has been dead for four days.

They lead Jesus to their brother's tomb to grieve.

"Take away the stone," Jesus commands when he arrives at the tomb.

"His body will smell too bad for us to go near it," protests Martha, because it's well known that bodies begin to decompose after three days, and smell. Horribly.

The disciples and the men of the village obey Jesus' order and roll back the stone that covers the entrance to the tomb. Word has spread throughout the village that Jesus is at the tomb, and now hundreds have gathered, curious.

"Lazarus," Jesus shouts.

Peter can't bear the tension and steps away from Jesus. To conceal his discomfort he absentmindedly grabs a long grass stalk and winds it around his hands. This time Jesus has promised too much, Peter thinks. The man has been dead *four* days.

Jesus with boldness yells, "Come out!"

Lazarus' sisters sob, worn out from false hope, then days of mourning. Then a uniform gasp erupts from the crowd and many fall on their faces in worship, as they stare at Lazarus, wrapped in his burial garments. His head is uncovered, and he squints as he steps into the sunlight. He is alive.

Jesus speaks again, but in a voice so loud and authoritative that it can be heard a hundred yards away. "Whoever believes in me shall never die. *Never!*"

Martha collapses in shock. Her sister Mary is shaking. John laughs, incredulous. Tears run down Peter's cheeks. "It's true," he tells Jesus. "You really are the Messiah."

Jesus turns and strides through the throng. Hands reach out to touch him, and voices call him names like "Lord" and "the King."

Peter runs after him. John follows.

"Lord," Peter yells, "where are you going?"

"It's time, Peter," Jesus tells him.

"Time for what?"

"How long have we walked together, preaching my message?"

"Three years, Lord."

"Don't you think it's time, Peter, that we finally go to the one place that needs to hear my message more than any other?"

Peter opens his mouth in shock. He knows that Jesus is referring to a place where Rome and the Jewish high priests have total control. They are, in fact, walking straight into danger.

Jesus smiles. He stares at Peter. "That's right, Peter. We're going to Jerusalem."

CHAPTER THREE

BETRAYAL

It is the week before Passover, that holy day that marks the time in Jewish history when its people were spared from death and led out of slavery from Egypt. Ironically, they celebrate their freedom from past oppressors, while suffering under the yoke of new pagan masters—the Romans. It seems to never end.

Right now, even as all of Israel prepares to celebrate this most important and sacred occasion, one very select group of pilgrims is making their way to Jerusalem. Jesus walks at the front of the single-file line, leading his disciples and Mary Magdalene.

They are not alone on the dusty road leading into the city. Thousands of people walk dutifully in from the countryside and desert—children on their parents' shoulders, the elderly. Men pushing handcarts, women leading the family donkeys. Now and again the crowd parts to let Roman soldiers through, knowing that to obstruct their path might lead to a sudden act of brutality.

One family's cart has a broken wheel, and the cart is blocking the road. The wife grasps their small children and the husband desperately rushes to get the cart off the road before it blocks the oncoming Romans, but the columns of legionnaires are forced to come to a halt. Their commander, a decisive man named Antonius, takes control. "Throw it down the bank," he barks.

Everything the family owns is loaded on that cart, but the Romans follow orders and shove it into a ditch. The wife cries softy. The children wail as their precious belongings are strewn over the hillside. Then the couple notices one of their children isn't moving. The cart has fallen on their youngest daughter, and she lies crushed by its weight. As the devastated parents cradle their dead baby, the legionnaires move on. They don't even notice.

The pilgrims know this is no ordinary group of soldiers. There are too many of them, their shields and breastplates are highly polished, and they march with a precision and snap not usually seen in the Jerusalem garrison. They watch as Antonius gallops his horse down the line to a regal figure on riding a black stallion. It's Pontius Pilate. This impressive procession is made up of his handpicked soldiers. Their job is to protect him and serve him. They will stop at nothing to ensure Pilate's safety.

"What's the delay this time?" Pilate impatiently asks Antonius.

"A broken cart, sir. We pushed it off the road."

"These filthy people and their wretched festival," Pilate

responds. "Every year it's the same thing. I'd outlaw the thing if only Rome would allow me."

Pilate is returning to Jerusalem to take personal control of the city. As governor of this remote Roman province, it's his duty to maintain order during this potentially explosive period.

"How much longer?" asks Pilate's wife, Claudia. She rides alone in a horse-drawn sedan, fanning herself to keep cool in the midday heat.

"We'll soon be there," replies Pilate. The sedan jerks forward as the procession resumes its progress.

Claudia peeks out between the curtains. All she can see are horses' rumps and polished shields. She sighs and leans back, hating every minute of the journey to Jerusalem. Oh, that she could be back in Caesarea, lounging in her favorite chair. She hears wailing and sees the hysterical cart owner cradling his dead, bloodied child. Claudia, a believer in omens, recoils at the sight. Clearly it's a very bad omen to start their time in Jerusalem by killing an innocent child. "Nothing good will come of this," she mumbles, trying to shut the image out of her head.

For Jesus, however, the week is off to a rousing start. The people of Jerusalem have heard about him for years, and they now celebrate his triumphal entry into their city. He rides a donkey, which is most unusual for a man who walks everywhere, but it is the traditional way a king would come to visit his subjects if he came in peace. Hundreds of people line his path, throwing palm branches onto the ground to carpet the road. They chant "Hosanna," which means "save us," for even more than a spiritual teacher, these people hope that Jesus is the new King of the Jews. They believe he has come to save them from the Romans. "Hosanna," they chant. "Hosanna, hosanna, hosanna, hosanna." The roar is deafening, and Jesus acknowledges them all with a smile and a wave. The disciples walk on either side of him, somewhat dazzled by the excitement. This is their payoff for three years of sleeping on the ground and tramping through backwater fishing villages. Tonight they will sleep in a nice bed, eat a hot meal, and wash. The welcome is overwhelming for the disciples. This first big test of Jesus' popularity since he left Galilee is a success far beyond any expectation.

"Look at all the people," marvels Mary Magdalene.

"I never, in my wildest dreams, thought we would ever see something like this," John agrees.

Thomas can't believe what he's seeing, and even Peter, that most practical of all men, is dazzled. "This," he gasps, "is incredible."

It is also audacious. Jesus has chosen to make his entry

into Jerusalem on the donkey because scripture foretells that the King of the Jews will enter Jerusalem as a humble man riding on a donkey. The symbolism is not lost on the crowd, who know their scripture well.

"It is written!" they cry in the midst of their hosannas, clapping and chanting and waving palm fronds as a sign of fealty. Their faces are alight with hope as they imagine the day when they will throw off the Roman yoke. This is the One, the man who will bring a new peaceful age, free from poverty and suffering.

Peter acts as a human shield as the crowd grows more and more fanatic. He is fearful that someone will be trampled under the donkey's hooves.

"Hosanna! Hosanna!"

"Save us! Save us!"

It is written.

"Hosanna."

"A donkey?" Caiaphas, leader of the Sanhedrin, fumes when a servant tells him of Jesus' mode of transportation.

The elders of the Temple stand with him, shaking their heads. Jesus' arrival represents a direct challenge to the Jewish authorities. Claims that Jesus is the Messiah have outraged and incensed the Sanhedrin, the Sadducees, and the

Pharisees. Only they can anoint the new Messiah, and this carpenter from Nazareth is clearly not such a man.

"'See your king comes to you,'" Caiaphas sarcastically quotes from scripture. "'Triumphant and victorious, humble and riding on a donkey.'"

The elders say nothing.

"And where is he headed?" Caiaphas asks the servant.

The servant lowers his head. What he's about to say next will not be the words that Caiaphas or the elders want to hear.

"The Temple," he says.

"The Temple!"

One of the elders, a man named Nicodemus, quotes another verse: "'To lead his people to victory and throw out the oppressors.'"

"The crowds," Caiaphas demands of the servant. "How are they responding?"

The servant's name is Malchus. He had hoped to impress the Sanhedrin by racing to tell them Jesus' whereabouts. Yet it seems that every word that comes from his mouth is just another variation of bad news. So he says nothing.

Caiaphas knows precisely what that means. He paces animatedly. "And the Romans," he says, worried now. "Have they made a move against this man yet?"

Malchus shakes his head.

"Not yet," says a concerned Caiaphas, who remembers

only too well the massacre of his people. "We don't need Pilate feeling threatened, or intervening in this situation, particularly during Passover. If we have a repeat of those executions there's no telling what kind of anarchy will erupt."

Nicodemus agrees. "Last time Pilate felt threatened, hundreds of Jews were killed by the Romans," he says, stating what everyone in the room knows all too well.

Caiaphas nods to Nicodemus. "Go with Malchus. If he enters the Temple, you watch him. I want to know every move he makes."

———

Jesus urges his donkey on toward the Temple's outer wall. Peter, John, and the other disciples quicken their pace to keep up. The crowd continues chanting as they part to let Jesus through. The apostles grow tense as they realize that the people are expecting amazing things from Jesus. This time it's not miracles, but a complete revitalization of Israel. "It is written," voices cry out from the crowd. "He will be called 'Wonderful Counselor, Mighty God, Everlasting Father, Prince of Peace.'"

Jesus would normally shy away from such profound benedictions. Instead, much to the apostle's shock, he is riding straight for the heart of his own people's national identity: the Temple of Jerusalem. This can mean just one thing: the situation is about to explode. John scans the crowd nervously and sees for the first time that their actions are being monitored. He sees the hard eyes of spies and messengers, their faces bereft of the joy possessed by so many others in the crowd. Peter's eyes dart from face to face. He sees Nicodemus in his priestly robes, strategically analyzing their progress. Then, as he glances down a side street, Peter's heart sinks at the sight of Roman soldiers following them on foot.

A manic thug bursts from the crowd. His name is Barabbas, and as he leaps directly in front of Jesus, he yells the word "Messiah." He does not speak with reverence. Rather, he taunts Jesus, forcing Peter to move quickly to protect Jesus. He grabs at Barabbas's robe, which falls back to reveal the hilt of a long knife.

But Barabbas is too strong for even the rugged Peter. He shakes him off and gets close to Jesus. "If you're the Messiah, then confront the Roman scum. Prove it." All Jews want freedom from Roman rule, but anarchists like Barabbas believe that God wants them to use violence to attain this goal. "Make us free," he challenges Jesus, even as Peter once again tries to intervene.

Peter, John, and Thomas work together to form a human shield. "We come in peace," says Peter.

Barabbas looks directly at Jesus, whose serene eyes lock with his. Then Barabbas stops talking, as if mesmerized. He lowers his gaze and steps back into the crowd. He doesn't know what has affected him, but he feels Jesus' gentle power.

At last Jesus reaches the temple. He dismounts from the donkey and begins climbing the staircase to the Temple's outer gate. Not even his disciples know what he will do next.

———

The Romans are watching his every move. One wrong step will surely prove fatal for this Jesus. They saw Barabbas, a known revolutionary, approach Jesus. Ready as always to crush any sign of political dissent, the Romans wonder whether or not Jesus might be a coconspirator. But there are no Romans inside the Temple complex as Jesus enters. The great palace of worship is filled with Temple officials and money changers. The mood is tense, a stark contrast to the reception Jesus enjoyed just moments ago. The disciples are concerned that things could get out of hand. This is a time to remain completely calm, not upsetting anyone or otherwise inviting trouble.

Jesus reaches the outer court of the great Jerusalem Temple complex—the Court of the Gentiles, as it is known. He walks ahead of the disciples. There is purpose to his every footfall and a determination in his eyes.

"Now what happens?" Peter asks.

"I don't know," answers John.

Judas is frightened. "I don't like the looks of this," he says in a hushed voice. His fascination with being a disciple has been wearing thin lately, and he's not as eager as the others to lay down their lives for Jesus.

"Stay together and we'll be fine," Mary Magdalene adds firmly.

All around them, the great court is filled with human activity. Lambs, doves, and goats are for sale, and their sounds and smells add to the human cacophony. There is the familiar clink of coins being counted and changing hands. The climax of Passover is a ritual animal sacrifice. Poor pilgrims traveling into Jerusalem from all over Israel must part with their hard-earned money to buy the animals. But their coins bear images of Roman emperors or Greek gods, images that are thought to be idolatrous by the Temple priests. So pilgrims must change all coins into temple currency. A portion of the proceeds from the exchange goes to the Temple authorities, part goes in taxes to the Romans, and the rest is pocketed by the corrupt moneylenders, who prey on the pilgrims by charging more than the law allows for making the currency exchange.

The disciples stay close as Jesus stops walking and studies all that is going on around him. His face and eyes are the picture of sadness. He sees more than just animals and money changers: an old man being shooed away by an angry moneylender, a poor family trying to buy a lamb but having only enough for doves, a frail old woman being jostled, and a lost little girl crying. The commotion makes it impossible for anyone to engage in devout prayer. Jesus' face clouds with anger and resentment. He walks calmly toward the stall where the moneylenders have set up shop. Coins are piled on the tables. Their hands are dirty from counting money. They banter with one another. Jesus grabs the table edge with two hands and flips it over. Then he goes on to the next table and does the same. All heads in the Temple court turn to the sound of spilling coins, and onlookers immediately race to scoop up the fallen money. "What are you doing?" shrieks one money changer.

"Rabbi!" Judas pleads, scooping up some coins in his palm. "No!"

But Jesus is not done. He cannot be stopped. On to the next table.

Jesus flips another table, which bounces against a birdcage and sets loose a flock of doves.

Judas sees a band of Roman soldiers lining up like riot police near the entrance to the Temple complex. "Jesus! Please!" Judas pleads. He doesn't have the stomach for Jesus' brand of revolution. Judas wants to be safe and protected. He fears he will be thrown into prison along with Jesus and all the disciples. Unlike the other disciples, he is an educated man who knows the way of the big city. "If only you would listen to me," laments Judas.

But Jesus doesn't listen to Judas. He isn't listening to anyone. Another table gets flipped.

"Why?" asks one vendor, disconsolate about all his earnings scattered about the Temple floor. "Why have you done this?"

"Is it not written?"

"What on earth could you possibly mean?"

"Is it not written?" Jesus repeats, but this time in a booming voice that echoes throughout the chamber. In an instant, the entire court is silent.

"My house . . . My house shall be called a house of prayer," Jesus continues. "But you have turned it into a den of thieves."

Peter and John hold back the angry merchants as they attempt to punish Jesus, who has finished this task and is marching out of the court. In his wake are tipped tables, angry traders, and a scene of total chaos.

Nicodemus from the Sanhedrin steps forward. Judas is so impressed by his expensive robes that he almost trips over himself in his hurry to bow down to the temple elder.

"Who are you to tell us this? How dare you. It is *we* who interpret God's law—not you."

"You're more like snakes than teachers of the law," Jesus replies in a heated tone.

Nicodemus is beyond shocked. "Wait. You can't say that! We uphold the law. We serve God."

"No," Jesus replies. "You pray lofty prayers. You strut about the Temple, impressed by your own piety. But you are just hypocrites."

Nicodemus is stunned. Men of his rank are simply not spoken to in this manner.

Jesus reaches out and gently lifts the fine material of Nicodemus' robe, rubbing the fine threads between his fingers. "It is much harder for a rich person to enter the Kingdom of God than it is for a camel to go through the eye of a needle," Jesus tells him, letting go of the robe.

Everyone in the temple has heard Jesus' words. The Jewish pilgrims who have traveled so far to be here for Passover are inspired by such a courageous stance against the rich and powerful men of the religious establishment, who have oppressed their own people as much as the Romans have. Only they've used threats and God's law to control the people instead of brute force.

Nicodemus looks about uneasily. He feels trapped. The crowd is definitely on Jesus' side. At the far end of the chamber, he sees the Roman soldiers prepared to move in if the situation gets out of hand. Such an intervention would further discredit the Temple elders and Sanhedrin, so Nicodemus says nothing as Jesus strolls away. He will deal with Jesus another day.

Nicodemus notices that one of the disciples, Judas, seems more impressed by the ways of the Temple than by Jesus. He calmly eyes the man, and is rewarded with a deferential gaze.

"Messiah," the crowd chants spontaneously, as Jesus continues on his way out of the Temple. "Messiah!"

Jesus shows no fear as he walks past the line of Roman soldiers at the entrance, their shields braced for signs of trouble.

———

Jesus' actions in the Temple have confirmed Caiaphas's worst fears. He and a handful of elders have been watching the action from a balcony high above the Temple floor. The chant of the crowd still vibrates throughout the great chamber long after Jesus has left. The people have been energized by Jesus. That makes the elders very nervous.

"This is outrageous," fumes Caiaphas. He normally prides himself on his stoic behavior, preferring to come across as unruffled and untroubled at all times. So for his peers to see Caiaphas looking upset is extremely troubling.

A slightly breathless Nicodemus comes up the steps and joins them.

"You weren't much help," says Caiaphas.

"He's clever," Nicodemus counters. "The crowd worships him. There's something unusual about him that is easy for people to draw near."

"There's absolutely nothing unusual about him," Caiaphas snaps. "Except for his ability to create havoc."

Caiaphas turns back to view the scene. Just in time to see one of the disciples approach his favorite servant, Malchus. There is an exchange between them. At first Caiaphas fears that their words will be angry, but whatever this particular disciple is saying surprises Malchus. The two clearly reach an agreement and then part ways. As the disciple hurries to catch up with Jesus, Malchus cranes his head upward to where Caiaphas stands. The look on his face is all Caiaphas needs to see. Judas will betray Jesus.

Caiaphas turns to the elders. "We may have found a way to deal with this Jesus."

———

As he leaves the temple, Jesus is followed by the disciples, a crowd of excited new followers, and a few Jewish elders who want to know more about Jesus' teachings. Malchus trails far behind, working as Caiaphas's spy.

Jesus leads this unlikely procession of old friends, new friends, elders, and a spy down the Temple steps, then suddenly stops, turns, and faces them.

Malchus does his best to appear as if he's there accidentally, but his purpose is now clear.

Jesus ignores him. Instead, despite the huge crowd, he

speaks to his disciples as if no one else is there. "Do you see this great building?" he tells them. "I tell you that not one stone of this place will be left standing."

Peter and John look at one another. Did Jesus really say what they thought he said? Is he really threatening to destroy the Temple?

A Jewish elder has heard Jesus' words and questions him. "Who are you to say these things?"

Jesus continues talking to his disciples: "Destroy this Temple and I will build it again in three days."

"But it took forty-six years to build," replies the shocked elder. "How is this possible?"

Jesus doesn't answer him. He abruptly turns and continues on his way, leaving his disciples scratching their heads about what Jesus means by his comments.

"What does he mean?" asks the one they call Thomas, the one who is constantly so doubtful. "Destroy the Temple? I don't get it."

John has a gift for vision and insight that is unparalleled among the disciples. "He's saying that we don't need a stone temple to worship in. *He* will be our access to God."

"Really?" Thomas questions him, once again showing his unerring ability to question every little fact.

With that, John and Thomas hurry to catch up with Jesus.

Pontius Pilate's Jerusalem residence is far more sumptuous than his home in Caesarea, which is a good thing, because he rarely feels comfortable venturing outside when he's in Jerusalem. The city is totally Jewish, which is in stark contrast to the Roman design and Roman population of Caesarea. He feels like a complete foreigner when in Jerusalem, living in a small world with a completely different set of rules and way of life.

As Pilate and his wife Claudia take lunch on the veranda, Antonius, his top military commander, enters and salutes. News of Jesus' confrontation with the money changers spread through Jerusalem in a matter of minutes, but it's only now that Pilate is about to hear of Jesus for the first time.

"We are eating," barks Pilate.

"So sorry to bother you, sir. But a Jew has been causing trouble in the Temple."

"You interrupt our meal for that?"

"Sir, he attacked the money changers and said he will destroy the Temple."

Pilate laughs. It is the first time Antonius has ever seen Pilate laugh, and the sight makes him uncomfortable. "He has a very large number of supporters," Antonius hastens to add.

Pilate's smile disappears. "What's his name?" he asks.

"They call him Jesus of Nazareth."

This catches Claudia's attention. "My servants talk about him," she says.

Pilate looks at her quizzically and then back to Antonius. He has made up his mind. "This Jesus is Caiaphas's business, not mine. But keep your eye on these crowds following him. If they get out of hand, I will shut down the Temple, festival or no festival.

"I mean it."

———

Caiaphas and the high priests are gathered, discussing the situation with Nicodemus, his servant Malchus, and his handpicked group of elders.

"He said what?" asks an incredulous Caiaphas.

Malchus is the first to reply: "That he would destroy the Temple."

"I am shocked. He claims to be a man of God, and then says he plans to destroy the House of our Lord?"

Caiaphas remains silent, steadying himself against the shock waves pounding his body. This is far worse than he thought. Finally, he speaks. "We must act fast. Very fast. But with care. We cannot arrest him openly. His supporters will riot, and then Pontius Pilate will crack down." Caiaphas pauses, thinking through a new plan. "We must arrest him quietly at night. Before Passover. Malchus, what was the name of that friend of his, the one who approached you?"

"Judas, High Priest?"

"Yes, Judas. Bring him here. Discreetly."

Malchus nods and makes a hasty exit.

———

Jesus and his disciples camp on the hillside of the Mount of Olives, surrounded by pilgrims who have made their way to Jerusalem for the Holy Day. Smoke from the many campfires rises into the evening sky, and row upon row of tents cover the hill. Jesus drinks water from a small stream, as Peter tries in vain to gather the disciples to have a discussion.

"Has anyone seen Judas?" Peter asks aloud.

They all shake their heads. Jesus looks to Peter but doesn't offer an answer.

A figure steps out of the coming darkness and cautiously approaches Jesus.

"Judas," Peter calls, seeing a shadow by the olive trees, "is that you?"

A man whose face is covered by a hood steps into the light of the campfire. He wears a discreet cloak covering his temple robes. When he pulls back his hood, the face of Nicodemus is revealed. Nicodemus is a member of the Sanhedrin and a Pharisee, but he has come down under the cover of night to see for himself what Jesus is about.

"What are you doing here?" Thomas demands.

"I think you're lost, sir," adds John. A man of Nicodemus' position would never normally associate with ordinary people.

Nicodemus appears tense, but then Jesus steps forward. "Welcome," he says warmly.

The Temple elder is clearly troubled. He turns over thoughts and well-prepared speeches in his mind, unsure of where to begin explaining why he has come. But Jesus' kind welcome disarms him, and he joins Jesus by the fire.

A full moon shines down through the olive grove. Nicodemus starts: "Rabbi, they say you can perform miracles. That you have seen the Kingdom of God."

"You, too, can see the Kingdom of God," Jesus tells him. "But you must be born again."

"Born again. Whatever do you mean? How is that possible? Surely we cannot enter our mother's womb a second time."

"You must be reborn—though not in the flesh, but of water and spirit. That which is born of flesh is flesh; and that which is born of the spirit is spirit."

A sudden wind blow Jesus' hair across his face and rustles the tree branches. Nicodemus looks up into the branches. When he looks back he sees that Jesus is staring at him intently.

"The wind blows where it wishes," he tells Nicodemus. "You hear its sound but don't know where it comes from, or where it goes. So it is when the spirit enters you. Believe in me, Nicodemus, and you will have eternal life."

"Believe in you?"

"For God so loved the world that He gave His one and only son, that whoever believes in Him shall have eternal life."

Nicodemus is torn. Could this be the Messiah? Or is this just another false messiah, a deluded individual claiming to be God?

Jesus knows his thoughts. "Everyone who does evil hates the light for fear that their deeds will be exposed. But those who live by the truth come into the light."

Nicodemus feels a great peace wash over him. The moonlight shines brightly, and the breeze blows gently.

Judas skulks in the shadows, his head and face covered with a hood. He is on his way to meet Caiaphas, and he knows it would be disastrous if he were seen. At the entrance to Caiaphas's palace Judas removes the hood so that the Temple guards will allow him to enter. Judas is led into Caiaphas's inner sanctum, where he immediately feels ill at ease.

"One cannot deny that he has followers," Caiaphas begins. "Especially among the less-educated elements of our society.

But you, Judas...why, you intrigue me. You don't seem to be one of them. Why follow this man?"

"I can't explain Jesus to you. He has power. It's hard to put into words."

"Power to stir things up? Or, perhaps, to cause trouble?"

Judas looks embarrassed. "He says things...things that other people don't even think, let alone speak."

"Things like destroying the Temple?" Caiaphas reasons.

Judas is extremely uneasy. "Well, I suppose that if he was the Son of God—*if*—then he could truly destroy the Temple. But why would he abuse the House of God? Surely the true Messiah would seek to unify Israel, not divide it?"

"Maybe we should just talk, he and I? Straighten things out."

"Jesus won't come here."

"Judas, your friend Jesus doesn't know—he can't possibly know—where all this will lead. If the Romans step in, the slaughter will be beyond belief. They have done it before, and they can do it again. It will be the end of our Temple—and possibly even our faith. Do you want that?"

Judas remains silent as the high priest continues his argument.

"It's important that you help," says Caiaphas. "A friend like you could lead him here—discreetly, of course."

And now the high priest gazes straight into Judas's eyes as he delivers his summation. "Help him, Judas. Help your friend. Save him from himself while you still can."

"And if I do? What's in it for me?"

If Caiaphas had any doubts that Judas's initial approach was one of betrayal, those doubts have immediately vanished. Caiaphas reaches over to a table, on which rests a small purse. He holds up the purse.

Judas swallows hard. This is a moment of choice. "I'll do it," he says. He grabs the bag, and the silver coins clink inside.

Jesus returns to the Temple the next day, performing miracles and preaching to the crowds. The Jerusalem crowds swell. The people are liberated and energized by his words, and use the term *Messiah* almost casually, as if it is an acknowledged fact that Jesus is Lord. The groundswell of popular support, particularly during Passover, terrifies the high priests and the Temple guards. At all costs, they must avoid a riot. They know what Pilate would do, for this would be viewed as a revolution. But the religious authorities cannot stop Jesus. He's too beloved, too charismatic, and too authentic for them to make a move against him.

The same cannot be said for Pontius Pilate. The fervor of the crowds at the Temple are unlike anything he's ever seen, and he's sure that the situation is about to explode into full-scale rebellion against Rome. He calls High Priest Caiaphas to his palace and makes it all quite clear: "Stop the disturbances or the Temple will be shut down. There will be no

Passover." The rage with which Pilate speaks the words is a reminder that he is more than just a random administrator, sent by Rome to govern the Jews. He is a soldier, a physical man of action who thinks nothing of spilling blood. His disdain for the Jews is complete, so giving the order to slaughter and crucify those guilty of dissent will be an easy decision for him to make. Pilate is the law in Israel. Caiaphas and the priests owe their power to him, and him alone.

Caiaphas heads straight to his priests, then addresses the subject that is on all their minds. "We can't wait any longer. It's almost Passover. We must arrest this troublemaker—this false messiah—tonight."

"And how do we know he is a false messiah?" asks Nicodemus.

The room grows stone silent.

Caiaphas resists the urge to berate Nicodemus in front of the others. "Has he fulfilled any of the signs of a true messiah, as it is written in our laws?" he asks coolly.

Nicodemus remains quiet. There is no sense arguing with Caiaphas.

"Well, Nicodemus," Caiaphas sputters. "Has he?"

Nicodemus holds his tongue. There's so much that he wants to say, and so many points he would like to debate, but not in front of the Temple authorities.

"He must be tried by our laws," Caiaphas demands. "Either we eliminate this one man, or the Romans will step in and destroy everything we have worked our entire lives for."

Nicodemus can't believe his ears. "Eliminate? Are you talking about executing this man?"

"What is the life of one deluded peasant when our people's lives are at stake?" Caiaphas asks, as he walks off leaving a stunned Nicodemus alone in the huge chamber.

———

On the other side of Jerusalem, the streets are calm and the night air cool, as Peter and Judas approach a small home and knock on the door.

"What does he want us for?" asks Judas.

"He wants us to take supper," Peter tells him.

"To eat together? Before Passover? That's strange."

The door opens. Mary Magdalene answers. She warmly welcomes them inside. "Everyone's upstairs," she tells them, motioning up with one arm. Mary remains downstairs as the disciples climb the stairs and enter a small room. A single long, low dining table fills the space. There is a place for each of the twelve disciples to sit.

"Rabbi," Judas asks Jesus, who seems to have something weighing heavy on his mind. "Why do you want to share a meal today?"

Jesus looks at him, and then looks around the room at the other disciples, but does not reply.

The group prays together, asking that God bless their meal and their fellowship. The unleavened bread in front of them is hot from the oven, and its fresh-baked smell fills the room. After the prayer, the disciples relax, reclining on cushions, tearing off pieces of bread. But before they can eat, Jesus stuns them with devastating news.

"This will be our last meal together," he says calmly.

They all look at Jesus, thick pieces of bread clutched in their fingers.

"What about Passover?" Judas asks a little too quickly.

"I will be dead before Passover," Jesus replies.

Stunned silence.

"What do you mean?" demands Peter.

Jesus doesn't answer, but John leans forward and whispers in Peter's ear. "Do you remember that discussion on the road to Jerusalem, where he prophesied that he would be betrayed, arrested, and condemned to death?"

John doesn't need to continue. Peter remembers. The thought fills him with dread.

Peter has given up everything to follow Jesus, and he has been as loyal as any man can be. The thought that Jesus might die crushes Peter's spirit and pierces his heart.

"Don't worry," Jesus commands them. "Trust in God. Trust in me, also. You already know the way to where I am going."

Thomas is close to tears. "We don't know where you are going. How can we know the way?"

"But Thomas, I am the way. I am the way, the truth, and the life."

The disciples are not all educated men. Like Peter, most of them made their living with their hands, and attended school only long enough to learn the basics. So this concept that Jesus is introducing is hard for them to comprehend.

Then Jesus makes it even more confusing. He tears off a piece of bread and hands it to John. "This is my body," he tells them all. "Take of it and eat."

John has tears streaming own his cheeks, but he understands. He opens his mouth and Jesus places a morsel of the bread on his tongue.

Then Jesus raises a cup of wine. "This is my blood. I will shed my blood so that your sins may be forgiven."

Bread and wine pass from hand to hand around the room. "Remember me by doing this. Soon I will go to be with the Father, but when you eat my bread and drink from my cup, you proclaim my Glory, and I am with you always."

Judas tears off a piece of bread. Thoughts of his thirty pieces of silver dance through his mind. He is torn when he vaguely hears Jesus tell the disciples to "love one another, as I have loved you." Judas snaps back to attention when Jesus shares a new morsel of information.

"But now I must tell you," Jesus says, as the disciples pay close attention, "one of you here in this room will betray me."

The wine is passed to Judas. He struggles to keep his composure, his eyes now riveted on Jesus.

"Who is it?" asks John. "Which one of us would do such a thing?"

Jesus tears off a piece of bread and passes it. "Whoever eats this will betray me."

All the disciples stare, transfixed, as the piece of bread is passed to Judas. "It's not me," Judas protests, holding the bread in his hand, but not eating. "Surely, I would never betray you, Lord."

Jesus' eyes stay fixed on Judas. Looking straight back at him, Judas takes the bread. He eats it and shudders.

The disciples are all staring at him with a look of pure horror.

"Do it quickly," Jesus commands Judas.

Terrified, Judas scrambles to his feet and makes for the door. A disgusted Peter chases after him, not sure whether he will beat Judas to within an inch of his life or merely follow to make sure that Judas does not carry out this betrayal.

But Jesus calls Peter back. "Peter, leave him. You will all fall away. Even you, Peter."

"Never, Lord. I am loyal. I would never betray you."

"Peter," Jesus tells him, "before the cock crows at dawn you will have denied knowing me three times."

Before Peter can protest, Jesus rises to his feet. "Come. Let us all leave."

Caiaphas stands tall in his palace with anxious Nicodemus. The high priest is in a calm and deliberate mood, while Nicodemus is deeply troubled by what is about to happen. The law says that a man must be tried in the light of day, yet Caiaphas clearly wants to condemn Jesus this very night.

"Judas is bringing him to us before dawn," says Caiaphas

"But the law does not allow it," insists Nicodemus. "A trial must be held in daylight!"

"And does our law allow riots? Does our law invite Romans to spill Jewish blood? You were there. You heard what Pilate said."

Judas bursts into the room.

"Where is he?" Caiaphas asks.

"I don't know." Caiaphas fixes a stare on him, and he admits, "But I do know where he is going."

Caiaphas points to Malchus. "Lead my servant to him."

As Malchus leads Judas from the room, Nicodemus confronts Caiaphas. "Why would he come here?"

"Oh, he will come, Nicodemus. One way or another, he

will stand before me tonight and account for his lies and acts of rebellion."

———

Torchlight flickers on Judas's face as Malchus, Caiaphas's servant, and ten men armed with clubs and swords walk with Judas. Judas is in way over his head, but even if he had doubts, it's far too late for that. The rogue disciple has no choice but to lead them to Jesus. He is on his way to Gethsemane.

"Where are we going?" asks Malchus.

"The garden," Judas says glumly. "We're going to the garden."

———

The Garden of Gethsemane is deserted, save for Jesus and his disciples, who knows the time to leave his disciples, and this world, is fast approaching. He has spent the last hour in fervent prayer, but if the disciples are anxious about Jesus, they have an odd way of showing it—curled up on the ground, fast asleep.

"The spirit is willing, but the body is weak. Wake up," Jesus demands after observing them for a moment. He needs them to bear witness. "Stay awake. The hour is at hand."

Peter has tucked a long dagger into his belt. He double-checks to make sure it is there, making quiet plans to put it to good use should anyone attack Jesus.

Jesus leaves them, walking slowly back up the hill, once again to be alone with his Father. He knows Judas is almost here, leading a group of men who will arrest him by force. To endure what is about to take place, Jesus needs strength. As he arrives atop the hill, he immediately falls to his knees in prayer, presses his forehead into the dusty ground, clasps his hands together, and prays: "Father, if You are willing, take this cup from me. Yet not my will, but Yours be done." He is beset by confusion because he is both human and divine. Sweat falls from his brow as if it were great drops of blood pooling in the dirt. He is wracked with human fear of the horrific beatings and great pain he will soon experience. He will die a human death and after three days, his body—the Temple—will be raised from the dead, so that all human-kind can be saved from the penalty of death. The divine Jesus knows, but the human Jesus questions and fears. Those three days seem so far away. The earthly Jesus pleads for God to spare him the suffering and death, a form of temptation, similar to when Satan tempted him in the desert three years ago. Indeed, Satan now lurks in the garden, watching Jesus cling to the hope that his life might be spared.

Jesus hears the sound of an approaching mob. Their torches light the base of the hill, and their manic voices cut through the night. Jesus' head is still bowed, as he now prays for the strength to carry out God's plan. Sweat continues to fall. Now that God's will is confirmed, resolve washes over him. Not peace, for what he is about to endure cannot bring the gentle calm of peace, just resolve. "Your will, Father, is mine."

Jesus rises from his knees and stands alone in the grove of olive trees. His disciples suddenly burst over the rise and surround him protectively. A line of torches looms in the darkness, marching steadily toward Jesus.

"The time has come," Jesus says to everyone and no one.

Judas steps forth and kneels down behind Jesus, as if in prayer. Then he leans in and kisses Jesus on the cheek.

Jesus does not feel anger or contempt. He tells Judas, "Judas, you betray the son of man with a kiss?" Jesus understands that Judas's role is necessary for God's plan to be fulfilled.

A furious Peter draws his dagger and races toward Judas, who tries in vain to escape. Peter stabs at him, but misses. Malchus arrives with the Temple guard, and Peter swipes the knife, severing Malchus' ear. "Run, Jesus," Peter yells. "Run while you can!"

Malchus spins away in pain, blood flowing down the side of his face. His severed ear falls to the ground, as a circle of torches surrounds Jesus and the disciples. Jesus calmly lifts Malchus' severed ear from the ground and reaches for his bloody head. Malchus flinches, as if Jesus means to hit him. He is caught off guard when Jesus defies his defensive stance and gently touches his wound. When Jesus pulls his hand away, Malchus is stunned and confused that the few moments of indescribable pain are like a momentary dream. His ear is healed.

"Take him away!" a guard shouts, as Malchus stands stunned, fingering his ear.

"Jesus," moans Peter.

"It is my Father's will, Peter. It must happen this way."

A horrified Peter watches as Jesus is shoved forward, grasped on both arms by strong men and surrounded by a half-dozen others, hooded, and dragged off.

The terrified disciples run off into the night, knowing their lives are on the line, fearing they will soon be arrested. Only Peter ignores John's pleas to come with him, and instead of running, he surreptitiously follows the line of torches down the hillside, desperate to see where Jesus is being taken.

Judas trails behind, as if in a trance, on the long walk in from the olive groves.

CHAPTER FOUR

DELIVERANCE

It is the middle of the night in Jerusalem. Jesus has been beaten. Blood pours from his broken nose. His body is bruised. His hands are bound and held by a guard. The Temple guards lead Jesus by a length of rope to Caiaphas, the high priest.

"Cover him up," cries Malchus. A heavy blanket is thrown over Jesus to conceal his face from the many pilgrims who support him. "Tell Caiaphas we have Jesus," barks Malchus as they lead Jesus into the high priest's home.

Judas follows the procession into Caiaphas's house. Malchus, however, places a hand firmly on Judas's shoulder and pushes him out the door.

"Not you," Malchus says with a sneer. "We're finished with you."

Judas walks off into the night, haunted by emptiness.

The door closes. Caiaphas stands waiting. The Temple guards march Jesus into the center of the room. Malchus removes the blanket covering Jesus and steps back into the shadows. Jesus and Caiaphas square off, though nothing is said by either man. The two are a study in contrasts. Jesus is bruised and bloodied, his hands tied together, and his simple yet elegant clothing dirty and torn. Caiaphas wears fine colorful robes, his body clean. Caiaphas looks into Jesus' eyes and is momentarily frozen. That gaze will haunt Caiaphas for the rest of his days. Caiaphas postures, an attempt to regain his lost authority, as Jesus stands alone, not a friend in the room, surreally in command as he awaits the inevitable.

Nicodemus and the elders enter the room. Because he has been beaten so badly, Jesus' face is horribly disfigured. Nicodemus and some of the elders gasp at the horrific sight. "You can't go through with this," Nicodemus tells Caiaphas. "This is not legal. Our laws say that a capital trial should be held in court, in daylight, and in public."

"This is necessary," Caiaphas fires back.

"Why the rush?"

Caiaphas turns on Nicodemus. His rage is a mixture of envy and anxiety. "You heard what Pilate said," he snarls. "He'll shut down the Temple if there's any more disruption. We must be rid of this Jesus—or God will punish us all."

"But what if he really is who he says he is?" asks Nicodemus. "What if he *is* the Messiah?"

"*We* will decide that!"

"*God* decides that," replies Nicodemus.

"God's guidance will be upon us," Caiaphas replies.

"But how can it?" questions Nicodemus. "For God commands that we obey His laws."

Jesus is led by a rope down a long hallway to the room where his trial will take place. The elders trail behind.

"Let me remind you what the law says," Caiaphas lectures Nicodemus, as the two men walk together. "It says that anyone who shows contempt for the judge or high priest is to be put to death. Anyone . . ." They stop.

The two men size each other up, then continue on in silence.

The hostile courtroom is packed. In the room where Caiaphas normally spends time alone, unwinding at the end of the day, the elders who comprise the Sanhedrin have gathered for the trial of Jesus. Makers and keepers of Israel's religious laws, whatever these men decide is binding. The sun is about to rise. "Brothers," Caiaphas begins, "thank you for coming at this hour. You know I wouldn't ask if this was not such a serious matter." Then he waves his hand and cries with mock reverence, "The one and only Jesus of Nazareth."

Jesus does not look up or speak.

"Jesus of Nazareth," Caiaphas intones solemnly, "you are suspected of blasphemy. Now let us hear from our witnesses." Caiaphas beckons the first witness.

"In the Temple," says the man who steps forward, clearly intimidated. "He healed a lame woman in the Temple."

Nicodemus can't bear to look at Jesus. It's clear that this whole thing is going to be a charade. A second witness is asked to speak.

"He said he would destroy the Temple!"

"I heard him say that, too," chimes in a Temple elder.

Caiaphas points his finger at Jesus. "You would destroy

the Temple! How dare you. That is rebellion against the Lord our God. Tell me, how do you answer these accusations?"

Jesus says nothing. Nicodemus stares hard at him, willing him to speak up. But Jesus remains impassive. The outcome is already decided. Jesus gathers his strength for the ordeal that is soon to come.

"The witnesses' evidence is clear and unequivocal. My brothers, we have faced false prophets in the past and we will face false prophets in the future. But I doubt we will face one as false as this!"

The room fills with murmurs of agreement.

A new voice cries out, that of an elder. "A prophet brings us new words from God. Does he not?"

Nicodemus is stunned. Finally, someone agrees with him.

"If every new voice is crushed, how will we ever know a prophet when we hear one?" the elder continues.

Caiaphas is thrown off. He chooses to deflect the question. "You are right, Joseph of Arimathea. How will we? I will tell you how: we must listen and then judge. So I invite this man—this 'prophet'—to speak." He turns to Jesus. "Are you the Christ, the Son of God?"

Jesus' head is bowed. He remains silent. Blood trickles from his wounds.

"Nothing to say?" Caiaphas asks.

Jesus slowly raises his head. His body stiffens. He stands tall. He looks Caiaphas directly in the eye. "You will see the son of man sitting at the right hand of God and coming on the clouds of heaven."

"Impostor!" Caiaphas cries, ripping his robe open to seek forgiveness from God for hearing such words. "Blasphemer! We must vote and we must vote now!" Caiaphas is so enraged he has lost his senses.

Jesus knows the verdict and the sentence that will be read before the vote is taken.

Joseph of Arimathea and Nicodemus shake their heads at the sham, feeling helpless to stop it.

"The sentence is death," Caiaphas cries out.

"This is wrong," yells Joseph. "This verdict brings shame on this council."

Caiaphas ignores him.

Jesus' followers have gathered at the Temple, the normal place for Jesus to be brought, which is exactly why Caiaphas had Jesus led to his home instead. Disciples Mary and John make their way through the crowd of tents and sleeping, uneducated, largely unsophisticated pilgrims. The Temple guards glare at them, recognizing them from their many appearances with Jesus.

Mary Magdalene notices the distraught face of Mary, the mother of Jesus. She wanders through the crowd. They rush to her side.

"Mary! John! Where is my son?"

"Jesus has been arrested, but we don't know where they've taken him," responds Mary Magdalene.

"Arrested?" replies Mary. "At night?" Ever since that day the angel Gabriel told her she was going to give birth to the Messiah, Mary has known this day would come.

John glances around at the crowds. "He's not here. They must have taken him someplace secret. So they won't have any protests."

The sun rises low and red over the Temple.

The doors of Caiaphas's palace swing open. Peter is standing just outside as Jesus is dragged out. Throughout the night, his own life has been in jeopardy as he has waited to hear what has happened to Jesus, hoping somehow he can help.

Others have come to stand outside Caiaphas's door, as word of Jesus' arrest has quickly traveled. This crowd of supporters is devastated by the sight of Jesus' battered body, with blood caked on his face and bruises around his eyes.

Malchus reads from a proclamation: "Let it be known that Jesus of Nazareth has been tried by the supreme court of Temple elders. He has been found guilty of blasphemy and threatening to destroy the Temple. The sentence is death."

The crowd gasps. Judas, who has remained outside all night long, hurls the bag of silver at Malchus. "Take back your money!" he screams, distraught. This is not at all what he intended. The coins clatter to the cobblestones, at the feet of Malchus.

A large guard approaches Peter. "You . . . I know you."

Peter doesn't scare easily. "I don't know what you're talking about."

"You know him," says the guard, grabbing at Peter. "I saw you call him Rabbi."

"No," says Peter. "He's nothing to do with me."

"He's one of them," a woman screams, pointing at Peter.

He spins around and confronts her. "I tell you, I don't know him."

Peter sees Jesus being hauled away, and he is frustrated by his inability to help Jesus, who means so much to him. The rooster crows, and Peter remembers Jesus' words that he would deny knowing his beloved friend and teacher before dawn. The rough, gruff man sobs in agony. He looks for Jesus, summoning all his courage. Peter means to approach Jesus, even though he is surrounded by guards, and make his apologies— even die trying to free him from the guards. But he searches in vain. The Temple guards have already taken Jesus away.

"Where is my son?" asks Mary. She stands over Peter. The crowd has dispersed, and she has found the sobbing fisherman lying alone the gutter.

"They've condemned him."

Mary gasps in shock.

"They've taken him. I don't know where, but he's gone." Peter slowly rises to his feet, aided by John. A look of humiliation is etched across Peter's face. John notices but says nothing to his friend.

"I told them I didn't know him," Peter says, inconsolable. He breaks away and disappears down the street.

Mother Mary sinks to the ground, as the sun glints off the high walls of the temple complex. Her mother's heart clearly understands that the break of day brings little new hope. The disciples are broken and powerless against the authority of the high priest.

But Caiaphas is having problems. As he changes into his special ornate Passover robes, Caiaphas knows that he cannot execute Jesus, for such a public execution by the Jewish high council will enrage Jesus' followers and create just the kind of disruption he wants to avoid. But the Romans can do anything. "I need to speak to Pontius Pilate," Caiaphas barks to Malchus.

Pilate stands before a washbasin in his residence. As he finishes washing his face, a servant hands him a towel. "Where's my wife?" asks Pilate. "It's past dawn. She should be up by now."

Just then, the maidservant of Pilate's wife appears in the doorway. "Master, come quickly. Please."

Pilate follows her immediately. They run down the empty corridor to his wife's room, where Claudia lies on the bed drenched in sweat and hyperventilating. He goes to comfort her.

"I saw a man," says Claudia. "In a dream."

Dreams are serious business to the Romans, portenders of the future that should never be ignored. "Tell me about this dream," says Pilate.

"I saw a man being beaten and killed. He was an innocent man. A holy man," she says, then adds: "A good man."

Pilate looks to the maidservant. "Help your lady back to bed."

Claudia resists. "My beloved, pay heed to this dream. I believe it is a warning."

"And why is that?"

"Because in my dream, it was you who killed this man."

———

The branches of a giant ancient olive tree swing in the early morning breeze as Jerusalem greets the day. Its gnarled thick branches rise to a lofty height. Judas Iscariot sits atop the branch that he has chosen, in a hurry to get this done. He has located a horse's halter. The fit won't be as snug around his neck as a hangman's noose, and he may struggle for longer before losing consciousness than with a rope, but every slow, miserable pain he endures will be deserved. Will God have mercy on his soul? he wonders.

Judas slips the halter around his neck. The leather is rough against his skin. He then loops the other end of the halter around a thick branch and tugs on it to make sure the connection is taut. He takes one last look at Jerusalem. Then Judas leaps.

Nicodemus exits the Temple, staggered by the hypocrisy and arrogance he has just witnessed. It is early morning, and the pilgrims camped on the premises are cooking their morning meals, hurrying to prepare for the Passover feast.

"You know where Jesus is!" calls out a voice.

Nicodemus whirls to the sound. This is most unusual. The citizens of Jerusalem don't normally challenge a Temple elder. Nicodemus doesn't recognize the voice of John, the disciple, and keeps walking.

"Wait," John cries. "Please, we know you. You came to see him. I was there. You spoke to him."

Nicodemus stops and turns. "He's gone."

"Where . . . please. Please tell me."

"The Romans will have him soon."

"Romans?" John asks, confused. "He's never said anything against Rome."

"Caiaphas is going to hand him over to the Romans," Nicodemus explains with a heavy heart. "And there's nothing we can do to get him back."

As the stunned John contemplates what this means, Nicodemus walks on. For what he has said is a most simple truth: once a man has been handed over to the Romans, the chance of him avoiding prison or execution is almost none.

Pilate is tending to governmental matters inside the Roman governor's residence when Caiaphas is announced. The high priest is prepared. He knows that his next words must be phrased as precisely as possible.

"Prefect, we need your help," says Caiaphas. "We have convicted a dangerous criminal and sentenced him to death."

"And? When is his execution?"

Caiaphas moves closer, spreading his hands as if in explanation. "We—the Sanhedrin—cannot It's Passover, you see. Its against our law." Caiaphas punctuates his tale by bowing his head deferentially. Pilate looks at him with distaste.

"So do it after Passover," says Pilate. "Surely the man can live a few more days."

"Normally, I would say yes. But this man is an urgent threat—not only to us, but also to Rome. He claims to be our king, and is using that lie to whip my people into rebellion. This man could very well tear Jerusalem apart."

Pilate looks at Caiaphas. He wonders how such a pomp-
ous individual became the leading voice in the Jewish religion.
Pilate's patience with the man is at a breaking point.
"I am quick to punish criminals," he snarls, "but only if they
break the law. I need proof that this man has done so—or
Rome will not be pleased."

"He has broken the law, Prefect. I assure you," Caiaphas
replies.

"You had better be right," snarls Pilate, fixing Caiaphas
with a deadly gaze. "If you're wasting my time, you'll pay for
this." He looks at his guards. "I'll see the prisoner."

———

A ragged, bloodstained hood hangs over Jesus' head as he
languishes in the cells located within Pilate's residence. This
was once home to Herod the Great, who banished his own
sons to these same cells. Their fate, as decided by their father,
was death. The same fate befell John the Baptist. Now Pilate
will decide whether Jesus should face the same punishment.

The Roman governor enters. A guard pulls off Jesus' hood.
The Messiah slowly raises his eyes and looks directly at
Pilate, who is unnerved, just as Caiaphas was unnerved by
these same eyes.

"So," Pilate begins after a very long pause. "Are you the
King of the Jews?"

Jesus says nothing.

"They say you claim to be King of the Jews."

"Is that what you think, or did others tell you this about me?" Jesus replies calmly, for he fears no man. Pilate takes a step back and momentarily averts his eyes.

"Your own people say that," Pilate replies, regaining his composure. "So tell me: are you a king?"

"My kingdom is not of this world," answers Jesus. "If it was, my servants would fight my arrest."

"So you are a king?"

"You say rightly that I am a king. I was born to come into the world and testify to the truth; everyone who is of truth hears my voice."

"Truth? What is truth?" demands Pilate.

Jesus says nothing. He smiles and looks up into the single shaft of light that penetrates the dark cell. It bathes his face. The enraged governor feels like slapping the insolent prisoner—but something stops him in his tracks. He looks at Jesus for what feels like an eternity. Then he turns and leaves. There is something unusual about this prisoner.

Claudia greets him as he returns to his office. "Well?" she asks.

"They want him crucified," answers Pilate.

"You can't. I beseech you."

"Whatever for? This man is only a Jew. They say he wants to start a revolution."

"I tell you, my love, this is the man from my dreams. The

man you killed. Please don't do this. His blood will be on your hands."

"And if I don't? How will I explain a rebellion to Rome? Caiaphas will surely testify that it was my fault. If there is an outburst Caesar will blame me. He has already warned me once. He is not going to warn me again. I will be finished... *we'll* be finished."

Pilate walks to the window. His wife's pleas adding to the pressures of his office, pressures he's never felt before. He sees the pilgrims in the streets below, with their newly purchased sacrificial animals. Pilate starts to wish that he had stayed in Caesarea, if only to be away from that wretched Caiaphas and his political maneuverings. But if he had, this Jesus character might very well have caused a riot, and by the time Pilate responded in force, Jerusalem might have burned to the ground. It had happened before, and it could happen again. No... Pilate is glad he is in Jerusalem, determined to survive the next few days and return to his villa by the sea. But Claudia is right: Pilate doesn't want Jesus' blood on his hands.

Claudia places a hand on his shoulder, though she doesn't say a word, knowing that her husband often needs to focus his thoughts before taking action.

"Get me Caiaphas," Pilate says after a moment. "I have a plan."

Pilate greets Caiaphas and the elders with thinly veiled contempt. "I have met your Jesus and have come to the conclu-
sion that he is guilty of nothing more than being deranged.
That is not a crime in Rome."

"He's broken the law," Caiaphas protests.

"*Your* law," Pilate replies smoothly. "Not Caesar's." The
governor stares hard at Caiaphas. "Teach this man some
respect. Give him forty lashes and dump him outside the city
walls. That is my decree."

"Nothing more? Prefect, I cannot be held responsible for
what the people will do if you release a man who has broken
our sacred laws. Especially on this day, when our eyes are on
God."

"The people?" Pilate responds sarcastically. Pilate knows
his next move, even as Caiaphas tries to take control. But
Pilate speaks first. "Caesar decrees that I can release a prisoner at Passover. I shall let 'the people' decide which of the
prisoners in my jails shall be crucified, and which shall be
set free."

Caiaphas knows he's been tricked. He's too stunned to
speak.

"Send for the prisoner," Pilate orders.

A crowd is now gathered at the gate outside Pilate's

residence, peering through a large steel grate into the empty courtyard. Word has gone out that Jesus will be lashed. Many like to witness public brutality and revel in the carnival-like proceedings that accompany a good beating.

Jesus is dragged into the courtyard by two Roman soldiers. His face is crusted in blood, and his eyes are now swollen shut by a fresh round of beatings.

Mary, his mother, gasps. She stands outside in the crowd, peering into the courtyard through the grate.

Jesus is tied to the whipping post. His robes are ripped from his back, exposing the flesh. The soldiers now retrieve their whips. A single lash is an exercise in agony, sure to scar a man for life.

Jesus is about to endure thirty-nine.

"They're going to kill him," whispers Mary to Mary Magdalene, her heart breaking. John looks down at the two women protectively. The two soldiers stand ready to whip, one on each side of Jesus. They will take turns. A third soldier enters the courtyard, carrying an abacus. It will be his job to make a careful tally of the blows and report back to Rome that precisely thirty-nine were inflicted.

Jesus looks across to his mother. Her pain is enormous, but his eyes lock with hers and she feels a strong connection with him. It is as if he is reassuring her and reminding her that this is how it must be.

The lashings begin. Jesus does not cry out, even as the

crowd gasps at the severity of what they are witnessing. The harrowing punishment and ordeal Jesus is to endure has been preordained. Isaiah, the prophet, once wrote that there would come a savior who "was pierced through for our transgressions. He was crushed for our iniquities. And by his scourging, we are healed."

From a window overlooking the courtyard, Pilate and Claudia watch the ghastly proceedings. She winces with each flay of the lash, but Pilate has seen many such beatings. "Its as if he knows this must happen," marvels Pilate.

One last abacus bead slides from left to right. Thirty-nine lashes are now in the books.

Jesus hangs on the pole, barely alive but definitely breathing. When his hands are untied, he does not slump to the ground but stands upright, beaten but unbroken.

Now he is taken back to the dungeon. The guards, never known to show kindness toward their prisoners—especially Jews—have been busy while he was away. To have this delusional Jesus in their midst claiming to be a king is the stuff of folly, and they can't wait to take advantage. One guard has woven a crown out of thorny branches. It is gruesome to behold, with long spikes sticking out at all angles. He now presses it down hard on Jesus' skull, drawing blood as those sharp tips bite into bone. "King of the Jews!" the soldier exults, bowing deep in front of Jesus, then dancing a little jig.

One of the soldiers who beat Jesus has just wiped the

blood from his hands. He drapes the crimson towel over Jesus' shoulders as if it were an ermine robe. All the jailers find this quite hilarious.

Pilate orders that the palace gates be opened. The crowds pour in, not sure what is about to happen. They know Pilate is allowed to release one man of their choice before Passover, in one of the many events held during Passover. They wonder who will be set free. Surely, Jesus is no longer a consideration. He has paid his penalty and has probably already been released. That's how the law works. So they wait patiently for their options.

Pilate has skillfully deflected Caiaphas's demand that he crucify Jesus, and given the final verdict to this mass of pilgrims.

Caiaphas remains undeterred, however, and is ensuring that the pilgrims allowed into the courtyard will vote against Jesus. The mainstream Jewish people are not given a choice in the matter. Malchus, his servant, and the Temple guards now stand at the gates, denying entry to anyone who supports the man from Nazareth. Scuffles break out as many in the crowd vent their frustration for being denied entry. They howl in protest—howls that are completely ignored by the Roman soldiers guarding the palace.

Mary, John, and Mary Magdalene are among those kept

away. They watch in disbelief as a mob of pro-Caiaphas sympathizers stand ready to determine Jesus' fate.

Pontius Pilate appears in an upstairs window and the crowd silences to hear what he has to say. "Today," Pilate begins, "Passover begins. Caesar makes you a gesture of goodwill through the release of a prisoner chosen by you."

A bald-headed murderer is marched into the courtyard, followed by Jesus, still wearing his crown of thorns.

"I give you a choice," Pilate tells them. "You may choose between Barabbas, a murderer. Or you may choose this other man—a teacher who claims to be your king."

Laughter and jeers spew forth from the crowd. Caiaphas, who now stands at Pilate's side, yells, "We have no king but Caesar."

Temple guards now move through the crowd, whispering instructions and receiving nods of agreement. "Crucify him!" is spontaneously shouted by members of the crowd who have remained silent until now.

Mary, mother of Jesus, is horrified. Her hands go to her face, and she covers her mouth in dismay.

Pilate sees the look on Caiaphas's face and knows that he has an answer.

"Decide!" Pilate shouts to the crowd.

"Barabbas," they roar back. "Free Barabbas."

Outside the gates, Mary, John, and Mary Magdalene all shout in Jesus' defense, as do many around them. But their voices cannot be heard over the roar "Barabbas! Barabbas! Barabbas!" from the courtyard.

Pilate is mystified. He looks at Caiaphas and then back at the crowd. "You choose a murderer," he tells them with a shake of his head, then holds up a hand to silence the mob.

"Do it," he says to his guards. The bewildered soldiers reluctantly unlock Barabbas's shackles. The crowd cheers; the insurrectionist's eyes are wild with delight.

"And this wretch," Pilate yells to the crowd. "What shall I do with him?"

"Crucify him! Crucify him!"

"Save him," comes the chant from outside the gate. "Save him."

"Crucify! Crucify! Crucify!" yells the courtyard.

Pilate silences the crowd. "How can you condemn this man and spare a murderer?"

"Crucify! Crucify! Crucify!"

"Very well," he tells them. "Crucify him."

Pilate reaches for a nearby bowl of water and washes his hands. This is a deliberate gesture, mirroring a custom of the Hebrews and Greeks to show that he is not responsible. "I am innocent of this man's blood," he says, hoping to shift blame.

Pilate knows Jesus is innocent and that he can prevent his death. He has the power, and should simply disperse the mob. But instead of standing up for truth, he is taking the easier route of political expediency. It is a dangerous time in Jerusalem, the home to more than a million Jews and less than a thousand Roman soldiers. Pilate cannot risk the sort of tumult, as it would make its way back to Rome and Caesar.

Pilate dries his hands. This crucifixion is no longer his affair.

It has been just six days since Jesus was welcomed into Jerusalem. Now he is to be crucified on a hill outside the city walls, for Jewish law does not allow executions inside the city. Two criminals will also be crucified at the same time.

Crucifixion—the act of nailing a man to a wooden cross—is the standard Roman form of capital punishment. It is brutal. A man can take days to die, hanging alone on the cross until he wastes away. To this heinous death for Jesus is added the torment of dragging the cross through the streets of Jerusalem. He staggers, trailed by a guard on horseback prepared to whip him if he falls or drops the cross. Many who were denied the chance to spare Jesus' life line the streets, forced back by a phalanx of Roman soldiers who ensure that no one helps Jesus escape.

Jesus is in agony as he struggles toward his death. His body is bent by the weight of the cross, and the crown of thorns inflicts a new burst of pain whenever the cross bumps against it. The many beatings he has endured in the hours since his capture make it hard to breathe, for his jailers have kicked and punched him in the ribs again and again.

Yet he sees everything. Both the sympathetic and not-so-sympathetic faces in the crowd. He also sees Mary, his mother. Jesus stumbles and feels the lash of a Roman whip as he falls. He reaches out to steady himself, pressing his hand flat against a stone wall. It leaves a bloody print. As Jesus moves forward to continue his grueling march, a woman in the crowd places her own hand against Jesus' handprint. She weeps; she knows who Jesus truly is.

The ground is cobbled, so the cross bumps along rather than drags smoothly. The distance from Pilate's palace to Golgotha, the place where Jesus will die, is five hundred yards.

Jesus knows he cannot make it. He spits out a gob of blood and falls to his knees. He drops the cross and crumples to the ground. Roman soldiers are upon him in an instant, raining kicks and punches on his helpless body. Mary races forward to save her son, but a Roman guard grabs her roughly and throws her back.

"Please," John says, risking his life by stepping from the crowd. "She's his mother!"

Tears stream down Mary's cheeks. The Roman guard steps toward John with a menacing glare on his face, but the disciple is undeterred. "Have mercy. Please!"

Mary can't help herself. She flings herself forward and falls onto her knees, next to her son. She wraps her arms lovingly around him in what will surely be their last embrace. Jesus' eyes are swollen shut, and he can hardly react.

"My son," Mary sobs.

Jesus forces his eyes open. "Don't be afraid," he tells his mother. "The Lord is with you." Repeating exactly what Gabriel had told her when he visited her as a young virgin. His words give her strength, and his look of love fills her with courage. She tries to help him up with the cross. If she could she would carry it for him, but she knows this is what he came to do.

Then suddenly Mary is pulled away from her boy. The soldiers whip the fallen Jesus, but it is clear that he cannot carry the cross any farther. A man, Simon of Cyrene, is chosen for his broad back and obvious strength, and he is forced to shoulder the cross for Jesus. Their eyes lock, and then their hands link to lift the heavy wood. Together, they share the burden. Step by painful step, the two complete the long walk up to the crucifixion site.

———

Back in his palace, Pontius Pilate continues his running battle with Caiaphas. Roman law dictates that every condemned man should have a sign placed on their cross to indicate their crime. Pilate dictates the wording for Jesus' sign. "Post these words in Aramaic, Latin, and Greek," he tells a scribe. "JESUS OF NAZARETH: KING OF THE JEWS."

"He was never our king!" says Caiaphas, who stands by the window watching Jesus' progress toward Golgotha. "Surely, it should read that he *claims* to be the King of the Jews."

"*The* king," Pilate corrects him. "It stays as I have commanded." He stares across the room, daring Caiaphas to respond. But the high priest says nothing.

The crowd thins as Jesus leaves the city walls behind. Mary, John, and Mary Magdalene walk to the side of the road as it curls steeply upward, just out of Jesus' sight but always there. This hill is known as Golgotha, or "Place of the Skulls," because it is believed that the skull of Adam is buried here.

Choking dust fills the air, and Jesus can barely breathe. He trips and is immediately whipped. He rises and then trips again. And once more, he immediately feels the sting of the lash.

"My Lord," cries a woman as she steps into the street. Despite the threat of punishment by the guards, she lovingly washes his face with a cloth. But when she urges him to drink from a small cup of water, the guards snatch it away and hurl it to the ground.

Jesus and Simon of Cyrene finally arrive at the place of

crucifixion. Simon drops the heavy cross and quickly leaves. Jesus, no longer able to stand, collapses into the dust. The Roman guards spring into action. Coils of rope are unwound and laid flat. Spades dig out the excess earth from the holes in the ground so often used for crucifixions.

"I want to see him," Mother Mary murmurs as she strains against the arms of a Roman guard who prevents her from getting close to Jesus.

Mary Magdalene sinks to her knees and starts to pray. Mother Mary stands resolutely upright, keeping a distant vigil over her son. John stands next to her, ready to catch her if she collapses from the stress.

Jesus is laid on the cross. The guards stretch out his arms and hammer nails into his hands. His feet are nailed to the cross, one over the other. The sound of his bones breaking fills the air, and Jesus gasps at each new burst of pain. After everything he's endured today, nothing hurts like the moments the nails pierce his feet.

Pilate's sign is nailed into the cross above Jesus' head: JESUS OF NAZARETH: KING OF THE JEWS.

To raise the cross, ropes are attached, one end to the cross and the other to the horse that will pull it to an upright position. The crack of a whip, and the horse walks forward. Jesus no longer sees just the sky above. Now he sees all of Jerusalem in the distance, and his loving mother standing vigil at the base of the cross.

He can barely breathe. His outstretched arms make it almost impossible to draw a breath. Jesus knows he will suffocate. It is not the nails that kill you, but the steady weakening of the body until it becomes impossible for the lungs to expand.

The cross is upright. Jesus hangs from it. The executioner's job is done. Those soldiers who crucified Jesus divide his clothes among them and cast lots for his garments.

Meanwhile, those who have watched the crucifixion step forward.

Mother Mary weeps with unbearable grief.

"Come to save others, can't even save yourself," mocks a Pharisee.

Jesus hears it all. He moans, and then speaks to God: "Father, forgive them, for they know not what they do."

The two criminals have been crucified on either side of him. The first taunts Jesus: "Aren't you the Messiah? Why don't you save yourself and us?"

The second criminal responds, "Our punishment is just. But this man has done nothing wrong." He turns to Jesus and speaks softly. "Remember me, Messiah, when you come into your kingdom."

Jesus turns to him. "Truly, I say to you, today you will be with me in Paradise." He grimaces in pain. The Romans may have finished their work, but they won't go home until all three of the crucified men are dead. Now it's just a matter of time.

Mary, John, and Mary Magdalene stand at the base of Jesus' cross. He is immobile and seems dead. It is now midafternoon, almost time for the start of Passover, just before sunset. The Roman soldiers know that his body must be taken off the cross by then, and are contemplating breaking his legs to kill him quicker, but they will not need to do that.

"My God," Jesus cries suddenly. "My God, why have You forsaken me?" This is the opening line of Psalm 22, King David's lament for the Jews and a cry for help. Jesus looks down at Mary. "Mother, this is your son," he tells her, referring to John as he stands at her side. "John," he adds. "This is your mother."

Mother Mary stands, silent tears running down her face. John places a protective arm around her.

Jesus looks away, consumed by the pain in his mortal body. He looks to heaven as a hard wind kicks up. A rumble of thunder sweeps across the land. "I thirst," Jesus says. In response, a soldier soaks a sponge and raises it up to his lips on a spear.

Peter hears the thunder, as he sits alone in the room where his last supper with Jesus took place less than twenty-four hours ago. His eyes are rimmed in red from exhaustion and tears, for he cannot forgive himself for denying Jesus. The coming thunder terrifies him, and he doesn't know where to run.

Pilate hears it, as he awaits sunset inside his palace. Claudia does, too. She's certain it's an omen that her husband did the wrong thing by killing Jesus, and is furious at him. "I told you not to kill him," she hisses as the thunder breaks.

"Hardly the first Jew we've killed," Pilate responds. He lies facedown on a bench, his torso bare and a towel around his waist as a servant rubs oil into his back.

"He was different," Claudia rails. "I told you that."

"Trust me," Pilate tells his wife, ending the conversation, "he'll be forgotten in a week."

Jesus, in a barely conscious fog of pain, hears the thunder. Black storm clouds now fill the sky as he knows that the time has come to leave this world. "It is finished," Jesus says aloud. "Father, into your hands, I commend my spirit."

The thunder strikes. This bundle of energy, vibration, and sheer power explodes upon Jerusalem. In the Temple, the great curtain is ripped in two, and panicked crowds race to flee the building, leaving their hard-earned sacrificial animals behind.

Mother Mary knows it is the signal that her son has died. She stares up at Jesus with a look of utter calm. All the pain she has been suffering is gone, replaced by the peace of realizing that her son will suffer no more.

The terrified Roman guards believe the thunder to be an omen, and they hurry to break the legs of the crucified so they can remove their bodies before Passover. They hastily grab metal rods and swing them hard against the two criminals on either side of Jesus. But they see that Jesus is already dead. To make sure, the Roman commander runs a spear through his side.

"He's dead," the commander confirms, pulling his spear out of Jesus. He looks across at Jesus' mother, then back up at Jesus, and slowly says, "Surely this man was the Son of God."

Normally, the bodies of the crucified are left to rot or are thrown into shallow pits. But Nicodemus and Joseph of Arimathea have secured special permission from Pilate to take the body down and bury it decently. Tombs overlooking Jerusalem are normally reserved for the wealthiest citizens, but Joseph has arranged for an expensive, newly hewn tomb to be the final resting place of the Messiah. Normally, a tomb contained the bodies of several family members, but Jesus' body would be the first and only body to be laid there.

The two stately elders, the older Mary and the younger Mary, and John gingerly retrieve the mangled Messianic body and prepare it for burial and, unwittingly, for its forthcoming bodily resurrection. His mother lovingly washes him with a sponge, cleaning away all the dirt and dried blood while the other Mary tears strips of linen. Mother Mary places one over Jesus' face. Nicodemus anoints each cleansed portion of the body with fragrant oils. Nicodemus prays over Jesus the entire time. Then the process of wrapping his body in linen begins. It is a long, emotional process, the official beginning of Jewish mourning.

A vast slab of stone is the opening of a cave, and Jesus' body is placed inside. The body of Jesus, immaculately wrapped in linen, lies alone on a hewn rock. Strong servants of Nicodemus and Joseph of Arimathea roll the rock over the opening of the tomb to make sure that the body won't be disturbed. Night has fallen, so the burial party lights torches to guide their way back down the path. As the group begins to leave, they are surprised to see a pair of Roman guards stepping forth to stand sentry. Pilate is fearful that if the body of Jesus disappears, all of Jerusalem will riot. Better to make sure it doesn't leave the tomb.

All over Jerusalem, the people are celebrating the Passover. But in the small upper room where Jesus and his disciples took their last meal, the mood is somber. The disciples expected the Kingdom of God to come when they entered

Jerusalem six days ago. Now everything they believe in has been destroyed. Their hope is gone. They have lost everything. They eat a small quiet meal together, certain that within moments Caiaphas or Pilate will send soldiers to arrest them.

The morning of the third day after Jesus' death, Mary Magdalene takes it upon herself to go visit the tomb. She misses Jesus enormously, and even the prospect of sitting outside his burial site is a source of comfort. Her eyes are tired as she ascends a small hill. She knows that even in the early morning fog, she will be able to see the tomb from the top, and she begins looking once she gets there. The entrance to the tomb stands open. The rock has been moved aside. She gasps. Someone has stolen Jesus' body. Mary fearfully takes a step toward the open tomb, but she doesn't dare enter.

Perhaps grave robbers are still inside, prepared to beat her for interrupting their labors. Then, an unrecognizable, distant figure standing on the ridgeline catches her eye. "Teacher?" Mary asks in a small and terrified voice. For a moment, Mary thinks she sees Jesus alive. But she can't be sure. Soon the figure disappears from sight. The fact remains that the tomb is open and the body isn't there.

Where is Jesus?

CHAPTER FIVE

NEW WORLD

Mary weeps at the empty tomb and then, still sobbing, takes a deep breath and conquers her fears. It's pitch-black, but her eyes soon adjust. She sees the slab where Jesus' body was laid. The linens that were bound tightly around his body now lie in a pile. Mary smells the sweet perfume that was poured onto Jesus' corpse to minimize the smell of decay.

"Why are you crying?" says a man's voice at the tomb's opening. "Who are you looking for?"

Mary can't see who's talking. Terrified, she finds the courage to call out from the darkness: "If you've taken him, tell me where he is."

"Mary."

It is the calm and knowing voice she knows all too well. Mary's heart soars as she realizes who is talking to her. "Jesus!" Her eyes swim with tears of joy and amazement as she steps out into the sunlight.

"Go and tell our brothers I am here."

Mary stares at Jesus in awe. She can see the marks on his hands where the spikes pierced his flesh. A quick glance at his feet reveals the same. There is an aura about Jesus, something far more heavenly than anything she has experienced in all their many days together. It is as if she is looking at two sides of the same being: God and man. Then he is gone. Mary, overcome with joy, sprints back into Jerusalem to tell the disciples the good news.

———

The disciples have been terrified since Jesus' execution that the religious authorities and Romans are working in unison to end all traces of Jesus' ministry—and that means snuffing out his disciples as well. They are hiding, fearful of that knock on the door in the dead of night telling them that they've been discovered.

Peter glances out a window. He is a shell of the man he once was, and no one would confuse him for the gruff fisherman Jesus recruited three years ago. Roman soldiers march up a nearby alley, breastplates and swords glistening in the early morning sun.

There is no knock at the door. Instead, a clearly delusional Mary Magdalene bursts inside, screaming at the top of her lungs, "I've seen him! I've seen him!"

"Close the door," barks John.

Mary slams it shut. "The tomb is open," she gasps. "He's gone."

"He's dead and buried," says a morose Peter. "That's impossible."

"You have to believe me. I saw him!"

"I think you were at the wrong tomb," mutters Thomas. "It must have been someone else."

"You don't think I know what Jesus looks like? Do you think I'm mad?"

"It's been a stressful time, Mary. For all of us."

This infuriates her. She grips Peter's wrist hard and pulls him to the door. "Come with me. Now."

Peter looks to John. Then at the other disciples. It wouldn't be safe for all of them to venture out, but perhaps maybe just two of them.

Peter nods. Mary leads John and Peter out into the sunshine.

They stare in shock and disbelief at the empty tomb. Peering sheepishly inside from a few feet back, they can't see footprints or any other sign that tomb robbers have been here, but they know that's the obvious answer.

"Thieves," says Peter.

"That's right: tomb robbers," adds John.

Peter steps closer to the opening. A white circle of light suddenly shines inside. Peter moves toward the light and sees the unmistakable Jesus. "My Lord," he says in a hushed voice. Peter reaches forth to touch Jesus. And then Jesus disappears.

A stunned Peter steps back out of the tomb. Mary sees the look on his face. "Now do you believe me?" she asks.

Peter hands John a strip of linen from the tomb. "But he's gone," John says, mystified.

"No, my brother," Peter assures him, that old confidence suddenly returned. "He is not gone. He's back!" An exuberant Peter takes off and races down the hill. On the way, he purchases a loaf of bread from a vendor.

"What happened?" asks Matthew as the three of them step back inside the hiding place.

"A cup," Peter answers. "I need a cup."

Peter gives a piece of unleavened bread to John, who puts it slowly into his mouth. "His body," Peter reminds him. A cup is found and thrust into John's hand. Peter fills it with wine. "And his blood," Peter says.

Peter, suddenly transformed into the rock of faith Jesus always knew he could be, looks from disciple to disciple. "Believe in him. He's here. In this room. Right now."

John drinks deeply from the cup as Peter continues talking. "Remember what he told us: 'I am the way, the truth—' "

Jesus finishes the sentence: " '—and the life.' "

Peter spins around. Jesus stands in the doorway. The disciples are awestruck as he walks into the room.

"Peace be with you," Jesus, the risen Messiah, tells them.

"No," says Thomas. "This is not possible. There is no way

you are Jesus standing here with us. This is all a fantasy, an apparition brought on by our insane mourning for a man we loved so very much."

Jesus walks toward Thomas and takes his hand. "Thomas," Jesus tells him. "Stop doubting and believe." He places Thomas's fingers into the gaping holes in his hands, and then to the hole in his side. Looking down, Thomas can clearly see the awful marks atop Jesus' feet where the spikes passed through flesh and bone, then into the wood of the cross.

Thomas doesn't know how to respond. He has traveled far and wide with Jesus, and he knows Jesus' voice and appearance as well as he knows his own. But what Jesus is asking of him is impossible. Thomas is a man of facts—a man committed to truth that cannot be disputed by emotion or trickery. He is being asked to believe that he is touching Jesus, as alive as the last time they all broke bread together in the upper room. It seems impossible. But it is real. This is Jesus, not some dream or vision. Thomas touches the wounds and hears his teacher's voice. Overwhelmed, Thomas looks into Jesus' eyes. "My Lord and my God," he stammers, tears filling his eyes. "It *is* you."

Jesus looks at his disciple with compassion. "You believed because you see me. But blessed are those who have not seen me, and yet have believed."

Faith floods Thomas's entire being as he slowly accepts

what it means to believe that anything is possible through God. This is the faith in Jesus that will transform lives. Not seeing and yet still believing.

Jesus soon passes on some sad news to his disciples: He is not here to stay. His work on earth is complete. He has died on the cross as a sacrifice for the sins of all men. Throughout history, a lamb has been slaughtered for the same purpose. Jesus has been the Lamb of God, who takes away the sins of the world. He has conquered death.

He appears to his disciples one last time before ascending into heaven. Peter has been fishing all night and pulled in more than 150 fish. The other disciples had spent the night on shore. As Peter pulled in his nets, Jesus invited them to share breakfast. When they were finished eating the small meal of bread and fish, he spoke to them of the future. He twice asked Peter, "Do you love me?"

The response came back as a surprised yes every time. And on both occasions, Jesus instructed him to feed his lambs and take care of his sheep. But when Jesus asked a third time, Peter was hurt. Peter also knew he had denied Jesus three times, so these responses were his moment of redemption. "Lord," Peter sighs, "you know all things. You know that I love you."

"Feed my sheep," Jesus tells him a third time. "Follow me!"

Jesus says good-bye to his disciples after forty days back on earth. For three full years he has trained them, equipping them with the skills to lead others to follow in his footsteps and worship God. "You will receive power when the Holy Spirit comes to you," he tells them. "My body can be in only one place, but my spirit can be with you all wherever you are. Go into the world and preach the gospel unto all creation."

The disciples listen intently, knowing that this is the last time they will see Jesus. He is not saying that the Holy Spirit will come into them right now, so they know they must wait for this great moment. Jesus stands before them and gives them peace. Everything he said would happen has come to pass, and it is clear that the power of God extends much farther than they even dared to believe. They have nothing to fear—even death. It is a proper and fitting way to say good-bye. Peter is anointed as the new leader of the disciples in Jesus' absence.

"Peace be with you," says Jesus.

The words echo in the disciples' ears. This peace pulses through them, infusing them with energy and calm resolve—this is the peace that will fortify them as they do God's work.

He then ascends into heaven.

The disciples feel the loss, as Jesus' physical presence among them is no more. Peter's eyes fill with tears. He tilts his head upward, as if squinting into the sun. Peter blinks away his tears and feels his breath return. He stands and addresses the disciples. He knows that Jesus will always be with them, and with all people. He has accepted Jesus' command that he follow him, no matter what the physical cost. Now it is time to go out into the world and let the people know about the greatness of God.

"Be strong, my brothers," says Peter, his voice sure and brave. "We have work to do."

With Peter as our leader we spread the word of Jesus throughout the world, shining the light on all creation. But with light there is darkness.

Persecuted for our preaching, all of the disciples die for our cause...except one.

I must live out my days in exile. Alone. On the island of Patmos.

One day I hope to see my friends again, for they are with our lord. I have been expecting death to come. And when He speaks to me I will listen, for His words are my fulfilment.

"I AM THE WAY.
THE TRUTH AND THE LIFE.
I AM THE ALPHA AND THE OMEGA,
THE FIRST AND THE LAST, THE BEGINNING AND THE END.
THERE WILL BE NO MORE DEATH,
OR MOURNING OR CRYING OR PAIN.
I AM MAKING EVERYTHING NEW.
YES, I AM COMING SOON.
MAY THE GRACE OF THE LORD BE WITH ALL GOD'S PEOPLE."

Amen.